'Just sex?'

'Yes.' Nell nodded. 'Just sex. And to be friends. That's all I'm willing to give.'

Ben frowned, looked almost as if he was going to argue, but then closed his eyes tightly for a moment before saying, 'Then that's what I'll take—and give in return.'

She put her hand in his. 'So it's a bargain, then?'

'Yes, a bargain.' Then the dark, hungry look came back into his eyes . . .

Dear Reader

Summer is here at last . . . ! And what better way to enjoy these long, long days and warm romantic evenings than in the company of a gorgeous Mills & Boon hero? Even if you can't jet away to an unknown destination with the man of your dreams, our authors can take you there through the power of their storytelling. So pour yourself a long, cool drink, relax, and let your imagination take flight . . .

The Editor

Sally Wentworth was born and raised in Hertfordshire, where she still lives, and started writing after attending an evening class course. She is married and has one son. There is always a novel on the bedside table, but she also does craftwork, plays bridge, and is the president of a National Trust group. They go to the ballet and theatre regularly and to open-air concerts in the summer. Sometimes she doesn't know how she finds the time to write!

Recent titles by the same author:

PRACTISE TO DECEIVE
SICILIAN SPRING

SHADOW
PLAY

BY
SALLY WENTWORTH

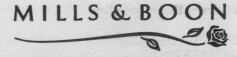

MILLS & BOON LIMITED
ETON HOUSE, 18-24 PARADISE ROAD
RICHMOND, SURREY TW9 1SR

*MILLS & BOON and the Rose Device
are trademarks of the publisher.*

*First published in Great Britain 1994
by Mills & Boon Limited*

© Sally Wentworth 1994

*Australian copyright 1994   Philippine copyright 1994
This edition 1994*

ISBN 0 263 78576 9

*Set in Times Roman 10 on 12 pt.
01-9408-54446 C*

Made and printed in Great Britain

CHAPTER ONE

'BUT that isn't fair!' Nell protested. 'After all, it was my idea to adapt the book.'

'And it was a good idea which deserves to succeed,' the producer said smoothly. 'You do want it to succeed, don't you?'

'Meaning?' Nell's face hardened even as she asked the question because she already knew his answer.

'Meaning that it will have a much better chance with someone who's experienced in writing for television, to adapt it.'

'I've adapted several books for radio,' she pointed out.

'But television is an entirely different medium.'

'I know I can do it,' she said doggedly, trying to keep the anger out of her voice, knowing it was useless, that he'd already made up his mind.

Max Elliott shook his head. 'Sorry, Nell, I can't afford to take the chance. But what I will do is to have you collaborate on the adaptation; that way you'll get some good experience so that maybe next time you'll be able to do the job yourself. How does that sound?' He grinned at her, expecting her to be grateful.

Stifling her disappointment with great difficulty, knowing that she had to keep him sweet, Nell managed a small smile and said tightly, 'I'll hold you to that.'

Max laughed, pleased that he'd managed things so diplomatically. Reaching across the desk, he patted her hand. 'Don't look so unhappy; your name will be on the credits and everyone will know it was your idea.'

Nell dropped her pen on the floor and took her hand from under his to pick it up. It looked perfectly natural but wasn't. Afterwards she folded her hands in her lap, out of his reach. 'Who were you thinking of to do the adaptation, then?' she asked.

'I'm not sure yet. I have to find out who's available. But I do have someone in mind, and if we can get him...' He made an expansive gesture, but then tapped his finger against the side of his rather long nose. 'But I mustn't speculate. I have to make sure first.'

'It's got to be someone good,' Nell insisted.

'Don't worry, it will be. I want this project to be a success for all our sakes,' Max assured her.

She leaned towards him, her chin thrust forward determinedly. 'And there's something else I want made clear.'

'And what's that?' he asked indulgently, willing to accede a point now that he hadn't been forced to fight and come the heavy to make her accept someone else to do the job. She'd taken defeat gracefully enough, and for that he was grateful.

'I want whoever does it to be quite sure that this is a collaboration, an *equal* collaboration,' she stressed. 'I'm not going to be there as some glorified secretary, at some man's beck and call. The person you're going to get may have the technical know-how for television, but I know how I want the book to be adapted. You know that from the comprehensive synopsis I gave you.'

'And it was the synopsis that sold the idea to me, and that's the way I want it to be adapted, too. So you've got no worries on that score.'

'But I might have on the other,' she guessed shrewdly.

Max shrugged. 'It's up to you to work out a working relationship with the adaptor. It wouldn't be professional of me to tell him how to behave towards you.'

He'd said 'him' again, Nell noticed, and was sure now that the person he had in mind was definitely a man. It was bound to be, she supposed wryly. 'But you will make it clear to him that this is to be an equal collaboration?' she repeated.

Max looked at her, wondering how a girl who had such striking looks could also be so intelligent. For a moment he was tempted to tell her to sort it out herself, but the book would make great television and he wanted her to come to him if she had any more bright ideas, so he said, 'It will be written into the contract.'

She nodded, satisfied, and got down to practicalities. 'How soon do you think we would be able to start?'

'All depends if I can get the person I want.'

'Haven't you asked him yet?'

'I've put out feelers to his agent,' he admitted cautiously. 'I gather there are one or two problems, but I should know definitely within a couple of weeks. I expect there's some work he's got to finish or something,' he guessed.

'Where will we work?'

'How about your place?'

Nell shook her head decisively. 'Too small and too noisy.'

'Well, if the writer doesn't have an office you can always use a spare one in this building. That OK?'

'Fine.' Her brown eyes filled with eagerness. 'I can't wait to get started.'

Max smiled, but said rather drily, 'Well, don't make a start by yourself; don't forget this is supposed to be an *equal* collaboration, and equal works both ways.'

She gave a genuine smile of appreciation at that, warming and lighting a face that, although attractive, could be withdrawn in repose. 'I won't.' She stood up. 'You'll let me know as soon as you know who the writer will be for sure?'

'Of course.'

Nell left then, and took the Tube to Broadcasting House where a children's serial she had adapted was due for rehearsal. There were a couple of hours to kill first, so she walked up the stairs to the first floor and took the lift up to the canteen on the eighth. Here she bought a coffee and sandwich, and took a seat at a table against the window where she had a fantastic view across the roofs of London, a view that never ceased to fascinate her, especially when the sun was shining brightly as it was today. But not all her attention was given to the view; she'd taken a seat facing the entrance so that she could see everyone queuing up for their food, and could wave to anyone she knew. When you were starting out on a rather precarious writing career, it was a good idea to see and be seen, to make and keep as many contacts as possible.

There was a book in her briefcase and she would rather have taken it out to read, to have sat with her back to the room and ignored everyone in it, but it was necessary to be friendly and outgoing. The canteen—it was now more grandly called a restaurant but the old name seemed to stick—wasn't very busy at first, but after half an hour a young actress who was in the serial came in with a friend. Nell waved to her, the girls came over and soon they were joined by two other actresses they knew. That was good; you learned things, not only about the serial she'd written from the cast's point of view, but about other productions the actors were in, and projects they'd heard rumours about where there might possibly be an opening.

Nell enjoyed chatting with the girls, especially when they talked shop, but got bored when they started talking boyfriends and pulling men to pieces.

'How about you, Nell?' one of the girls asked her. 'Who's your latest?'

'Oh, I don't have even an earliest, let alone a latest,' she said lightly. 'I'm far too busy working on my career and trying to earn a living.'

'And me,' said another girl feelingly. 'This is the first part I've had in three months.'

So they were safely back discussing show business again.

When it was time to go to the rehearsal studio, Nell followed them out. Anyone watching them might well have taken it that they were all actresses; Nell, at twenty-five, was older than the other girls, and although she was quite short she had a good, slim figure, and a bell of thick dark hair that curled gently at the neck. But it was her face that caught and held the attention; her eyes, large and long-lashed, were set wide beneath level brows and a high forehead, and she had high cheekbones that thinned her face and gave it elegance. They also, though, helped to add to the look of cool withdrawal that came naturally to her and which she often had to fight against. But here she was aided by her mouth, which had a full, soft underlip that gave an impression of unawakened sexuality and was an attraction in itself.

Sometimes, such as when she was trying to persuade someone to give her an interview, her looks were an advantage, at others, as today when she'd been trying to make Max believe that she could do the job alone, they'd been a disadvantage. Nell was sure that her looks were one of the reasons why he hadn't taken her seriously, and also that if she'd been a man he would have at least let her try to do the adaptation alone. Women might be gaining great grounds careerwise, but they still had to fight men's basic instinct that a woman, especially a good-looking one, wasn't to be accepted on equal terms.

The rehearsal went well; she only had to make one or two minor changes, and the parts had been well cast, the voices sounding right for the roles. Afterwards, she stopped to chat with everyone for a while, but then took the Tube back to her flat. She had lied about the flat to Max Elliott. It wasn't that small, and not at all noisy, but there was no way she was going to throw it open to be used as an office by some man she was against having to collaborate with in the first place. No, a neutral office in the television company's headquarters would be much better.

Taking a bottle of white wine from the fridge, Nell kicked off her shoes and sat down on the settee to drink a glass. Although disappointed that she hadn't been allowed to adapt the book by herself, it was still great that her idea had been accepted at all. It meant a couple of months of creative work, money coming in to pay the rent, and another credit to add to the growing list of programmes with which she'd been associated. All of which were on the plus side. And maybe Max was right after all, she thought generously. Maybe she would be able to learn a lot about the technical side of television from the man he chose. If she was lucky. If he allowed her to learn from him and didn't zealously guard his own expertise and experience. Which wouldn't be surprising; to teach her would be to create his own rival.

For a few minutes pessimism took over, but then Nell took another drink and determined to look on the bright side; today had been a relatively good one, tomorrow could look after itself.

It was over a week later before Max phoned. 'I've got the man I wanted,' he told her excitedly.

'Who is it?'

'Ben Rigby. Have you heard of him?'

'Ben Rigby?' For a moment she frowned in concentration, then her brow cleared. 'You don't mean Benet Rigby—the man who adapted the *Eastern Trilogy*?' she said on a surprised note.

'That's the one. And we were darn lucky to get him; his agent said he wasn't available at first. Then he changed his mind for some reason.'

'What did he say about me collaborating with him?' Nell asked anxiously.

'No problem. I sent him your synopsis and he's happy to go along with the adaptation along those lines.'

'Great! When do we start work?' Nell asked excitedly.

'He'll be free from next Monday. I've suggested he come along here at nine-thirty and we'll sort out an office and everything. Suit you?'

'Fine.'

'OK. Oh, and he wants a copy of the book so that he can read it through first.'

'I only have the one; it's out of print.'

'Well, lend it to him, will you, Nell? It's important he should read it.'

'Yes, of course,' she agreed, albeit with a strange inner reluctance. 'I'll bring it into your office so he can collect it, shall I?'

'No. He wants it straight away. I'm to give him your address and he'll send a special messenger to collect it. Will you be at home all this evening?'

'Yes, I'll make sure to be here.'

Max rang off, leaving Nell with an inner feeling of optimism. If the *Eastern Trilogy* was anything to go by, Benet Rigby must be really good. The series had hit the top of the ratings despite being a serious, and virtually sexless drama. Not the kind of thing the majority of viewers would be expected to go for, but the script and the actors had been outstanding.

Finding a padded bag, Nell carefully wrapped her copy, her only copy, of *A Midwinter Night's Dream* inside it. The book was old, early Victorian, thick and heavy. Its hard cover had once been covered with bright blue cloth which was now very faded and stained. The pages were of thick paper, their edges uneven where they had originally been joined together and parted with a paper-knife wielded by an impatient hand. Nell couldn't blame that first reader for having been so eager; when she'd come across the book, among a pile at a jumble sale that hadn't sold and were waiting to be thrown away, she had dipped into it and immediately become riveted, realising that here was hidden gold. The book was by J.L.T., just the initials, with no indication whatsoever of the author's sex. After she had found it Nell had spent a long time in the reading room of the British Library, trying to find out the writer's identity, but without any success. In some perverse way this pleased her; she liked the air of mystery it gave to the book. In her own mind she was certain that it was by a woman; surely only a woman could have described those love scenes with such feeling, such intimacy.

Nell pushed the thought of the love scenes aside, finding them oddly disturbing. She would have to think about them when it came time to put them into the script, of course, but love scenes were usually visual things and they would be quickly done. Until then she would forget them and the strange feeling of disquiet they gave her.

The bell rang and she ran down the single flight of stairs to the front door. Her flat was in a mews, above what had once been stables for a large house on the main road that had been converted into luxury apartments fifty years ago. The stables were now used to garage cars but Nell had been living in the flat above for the last two years. She opened the door and was taken aback to see a figure that looked as if it had escaped from the latest robot-cop movie. Dressed all in black leather motor-cycle gear and with a helmet with the visor down, the man was so tall he towered over her.

He had half turned away but looked round as the door opened. He lifted his hand as if to raise the visor but it must have been merely to shield his eyes from the sun. His voice was muffled and he said after a moment, 'Miss Marsden?'

'Yes.'

'I've called to collect a parcel.'

Reluctantly she held the envelope out to him. 'You will be careful with it, won't you?'

Looking at the powerful black motorbike that stood at the kerb, she noticed that there were no panniers showing the name of the company as she'd seen on all the other messenger-service bikes that were forever weaving their way through the London traffic. She went to ask the man where he meant to put it for safety, but he had already unzipped the front of his leather jacket and was putting the envelope inside.

'Are you sure it will be all right there?' He nodded, but she was by no means reassured and said sharply, 'I hope your company's insured, because if you lose it I'll sue.'

The messenger, so intimidating in his faceless blackness, looked down at her for a moment, making Nell feel physically weak and helpless, a sensation she didn't like, but then he lifted a hand, whether in farewell or acknowledgement she couldn't tell, put his legs astride the powerful machine, and roared off down the cobbled road.

Nell was at Max's office promptly on Monday morning but Benet Rigby was late. It was almost ten before he appeared, and by then Nell was annoyed enough to notice only that he looked untidy, as if he'd thrown his clothes on, and that he needed a shave. Or maybe it was supposed to be designer stubble. If it was it didn't suit him, she thought crossly.

But at least he apologised, if somewhat brusquely. 'Sorry I'm late. Domestic crisis.'

'Don't worry about it,' Max answered in what Nell felt was an ingratiating tone. 'This is Nell Marsden, who had the brilliant idea of adapting the book.'

'Hello.'

'How do you do?' Nell returned primly, still annoyed, and was rather surprised to have her hand taken in a firm grip and to be looked over by a pair of quizzical grey eyes as it was shaken. Max didn't bother to introduce Ben to her. 'Did you receive the book all right?' she asked anxiously.

'Of course.'

Her relief was tainted by the amusement in his answer, as if he thought her a silly, fussing female. Turning to Max, she said, 'Have you got an office in mind for us?'

'Yes, a couple of floors up. This way.'

They all got into the small lift, Nell standing next to Ben. She was wearing her high heels today which gave her several extra inches and usually allowed her to look most men near enough in the eye, but even so she only came up to his shoulder. She sighed inwardly, wondering if he was the kind of man who would use his extra height, as well as his masculinity and his extra experience, to try to browbeat her. Well, he'd soon find that his extra foot wouldn't do him any good, Nell thought determinedly, then almost laughed aloud at the mental image that thought conjured up.

Her eyes were still bright with inner laughter when they walked into the office. Ben's gaze swept round it and then turned towards her, but he stopped what he was going to say and instead lifted a questioning eyebrow when he saw her face. 'What's funny?'

She shook her head. 'Private joke.'

The office was equipped with a couple of desks holding word processors, a central table, filing cabinet and a leather settee against the far wall. It was well lit, too, with lamps on the desks and a large window that caught the morning sunlight. 'This is great.' She turned to Max and smiled. 'Thanks for arranging it.'

'My pleasure. Let me know if there's anything else you need.'

'How about a phone?' Ben suggested.

'Well, I can get one put in if you really want one, but I thought you'd rather not be interrupted. You can always use the phone in my office if——'

'I'd prefer a phone in here,' Ben insisted.

His assumption that she'd go along with his wishes angered Nell. 'I'm quite happy to do without one.'

Ben didn't say anything, just glanced at her, then at Max.

'I'll have one put in straight away,' Max said. 'Anything else?'

'Paper. Pencils,' Nell said, not to be outdone. 'A kettle to make coffee.'

'All in the cupboard and drawers.'

'A "Do not disturb" sign,' Ben added with what Nell thought was a faintly mocking grin.

Max laughed. 'Of course. I'll find one for you.' He rubbed his nose enthusiastically. 'OK, then, I'll leave you two to it. Keep me posted how you're getting along and we'll talk over the first draft of the first episode as soon as you come up with it.'

His going left behind him a silence that Nell didn't find comfortable. Determined to be businesslike, she took off her jacket and hung it on the stand. 'I'll take the desk nearest the window, shall I?' And she moved towards it.

But Ben shook his head. 'No, let's rearrange the place.' He walked several times round the room, like a dog exploring a new kennel, looked out of the window and adjusted the sun-blinds. Max's assistant came in with the phone and found himself helping Ben to move the furniture around. When they'd finished the settee was under the window and the two desks were in the middle of the room with their backs to each other. The phone was put on one of the desks, the one on which Ben dropped his briefcase.

Nell had been leaning against the wall, out of the way, watching with her arms folded, her indignation growing. 'Happy now?' she asked sardonically when they were alone again.

Ben shrugged. 'We'll have to see how it works. If we're not satisfied with the arrangement we can always change it again.'

'We?' Again her tone was sardonic.

Ben's eyes flicked at her and she braced herself for an argument, but he ducked it, merely saying, 'As I said, if you don't like it this way when we've given it a try, we'll move the stuff around again until we get it right. Is that what you wanted me to say?'

'No. I'd like to have heard you ask my opinion before you started throwing the furniture around.'

'I see. Stating your terms and conditions already, are you?'

'It would appear to be necessary.'

'Only if you feel threatened.' Picking up the phone, Ben dialled a number and when he got an answer said, 'If you need me you can reach me on this number,' and he gave the number and extension of the phone. Afterwards he dropped down on to the settee, leant back at ease, and put his hands behind his head as he looked her over. 'What's Nell short for?'

'Eleanor. What's Benet long for?'

He grinned at that. 'Ben. Unfortunately Benet is a family name that gets handed down. Usually it misses a generation because the holder can't stand it, but then sentimentality intervenes and it's used again.'

Crossing to the swing chair in front of one of the desks, Nell said, 'Shall we start work?'

But Ben only crossed his legs at the knee, the way men did when they were relaxed, and said, 'Don't you think it would be a good idea to get to know each other a bit more first?'

Nell didn't, and said bluntly, 'I don't see why; we can learn as we work.'

'Such eagerness,' he grinned.

'Naturally I'm eager,' Nell replied, trying to keep her voice light. 'After all, I've been working on this project for almost a year, writing the synopsis, trying to find a producer to take it.'

'You're telling me it's your baby, right?'

'That's right.'

'Until Max foisted me on to you.' Ben was still sitting there casually, his eyes almost half-closed, but Nell had the feeling he was watching her narrowly.

Her chin came up. She had no choice but to work with this man, so she supposed she'd better keep him sweet. 'He has great faith in you. He went overboard about your adaptation of the *Eastern Trilogy* and was certain that with you on the team we'd be absolutely sure of success. We were both terrifically pleased when your agent said you were free to take the assignment.'

'I can see you have a career in creative fiction ahead of you,' Ben remarked drily. His eyes ran over her again and he said, 'You don't look like a writer.'

Surprised, she said, 'Why not?'

'Too small, too feminine. Not tough enough.'

'Should writers be tough, then?'

'Oh, definitely. Especially women writers.' Adding, with irony, 'Strong enough to move their own desk around at any rate.'

She had begun to be amused, but didn't know how to take that. Instead she looked at him, openly assessing him. She'd expected Benet Rigby, getting on for famous, to be a flamboyant character, long-haired perhaps, semi-intellectual certainly, but the reality seemed to be none of these. Ben was wearing casual clothes, looked even a little unkempt, and although his dark hair was quite long it wasn't at all arty. Mostly he came across as what he'd said a writer should be—tough; his shoulders were broad and his chin masterful. He wasn't that old, but there were a few lines around his mouth, and shadows

of tiredness around his eyes. Maybe he'd lived it up too
well the night before, she surmised, and wondered about
the personality behind the face.

'And your conclusions?' he asked, perfectly aware of
her thoughts.

She smiled a little. 'You don't look like a writer.'

'Why not?'

'Too tough.'

'Ah... So we obviously have entirely different ideas
about what a writer should look like.'

Nell shook her head. 'No—we just look in different
mirrors.'

Ben laughed at that; a laugh of genuine amusement.
Different lines appeared around his mouth, and for the
first time she thought that maybe this unwanted collaboration might just work after all.

Maybe Ben thought so too, because he took her synopsis and the book from his briefcase and put them on
the table, drew up a chair. 'I like the book. I tried to
get hold of a copy, but there don't seem to be any
around.'

'No. I found out that it was published privately; that's
why there isn't a copy in the British Library.'

'Vanity publishing,' Ben commented. 'Somebody must
have really believed in the story to do that.'

'Or else have felt the need to tell it,' Nell said, coming
to sit opposite him.

He raised his left eyebrow, the one that arched more
than the other as if he was in the habit of questioning
what he heard. 'You think it's a true story? That's hard
to believe.'

'Stranger things have happened.'

'Yes, but for the love-affair to have gone on for so long without the heroine realising who her secret lover was? It's hardly credible.'

'Maybe in her heart she did know but didn't want to believe it. She didn't want to spoil what was perfect.'

'Perhaps you're right. It's certainly very sensitively written.'

'And that sensitivity is what I want to come over in the adaptation,' Nell said earnestly. 'I don't want this to be just another serial with explicit sex scenes—bare limbs all over the place and moans and groans in the appropriate places. This is a *romance* in the true sense of the word. That's the way it's *got* to be treated if it's going to be successful.'

'Are you implying that I can't handle that?'

She drew back, realising that her vehemence could have sounded like an accusation. 'Not at all. I've watched the *Eastern Trilogy* again; you handled that really well.'

'Again?'

'I got the tapes out of the television film library to watch last weekend,' she admitted.

'Checking up on me?'

'Doing my homework.'

Ben nodded. 'Fair enough. But this book differs a great deal from the trilogy. There's deep passion here as well as romantic love. Earthy, physical passion. That's what makes the book, and will make it interesting to the viewers. You can't cut it out.' He paused, waiting for her to speak, but when she didn't Ben went on, 'It needs to be delicately handled to combine the two, but I think we should be able to do it.'

Nell didn't comment on that, instead reaching out for the book. 'Shall we make a start?'

'OK. The first thing to decide is how many episodes.'

'Max said he couldn't get money for more than three of one hour.'

'That should be enough. It will give us an opportunity to express the length of time covered in the book. It's about twelve years, isn't it?'

'Twelve winters.'

'Yes.' Ben gave her an appraising look. 'You're very obsessed with this story, aren't you?'

'I told you; I've been working on it for a year.'

'And you've started to identify with the heroine,' he said shrewdly.

'You're supposed to identify with the characters when you read a book.'

'But not when you're adapting it for television. You have to have a clear mind; to be able to cut where necessary, not to be so involved with it that you can't bear to lose a line of dialogue because you're in love with the characters.'

It was said bluntly, almost rudely, and made Nell angry. 'I have adapted books before,' she pointed out coldly.

'I know; I did my homework, too. But never a full-blooded love story, have you?'

Her mouth tightened. 'I am *not* in love with the characters,' she answered shortly. 'The whole idea is ridiculous.'

'Good,' Ben said smoothly. 'Then you won't mind making any necessary cuts.'

She gave him a glare, knowing that she'd been out-manoeuvred. 'Shall we get on with it?'

His lips twisted slightly. 'All right. The next thing is to decide where the episodes will end. Now, the basic storyline is of a young girl, Anna, who is married off, in the mid-nineteenth century, to an older man she doesn't love, a man she finds cold both physically and emotionally. Not a rotter, not unkind, just unable to rouse any feelings in her. They don't have any children. Then one winter she goes alone to visit her parents but on the way back the carriage gets caught in a snow storm and she has to take shelter in the nearest house, which is inhabited only by a couple of servants who say that their master seldom comes there any more.'

Ben picked up the synopsis, glanced at it, then went on, 'They give her the master bedroom and the first night nothing happens, but one of the horses has slipped and hurt its leg, so she has to stay on. The second night she feels very tired, and while she's in bed she has a dream in which a man makes love to her. The most perfect, wonderful experience she could ever have imagined. The next day her husband turns up to look for her and everything is back to normal. But she treasures the memory of the dream, especially when she finds she is pregnant at last—but her husband hasn't recently made love to her.'

'She wouldn't have thought of it as making love, not with her husband,' Nell interrupted with certainty.

'No. The act of procreation, then. So she thinks maybe it wasn't a dream, maybe it was true. Anyhow she lets the husband into her bed, just in case, but finds his attentions even more abhorrent now—— Is that the kind of language that suits you?' Ben broke off to ask Nell.

Missing the slightly dry note in his tone, she nodded. 'Yes, that's how she would think.'

'OK.' He put his elbows on the table and pyramided his hands. 'The child is born, a girl, but the husband still needs an heir, which isn't forthcoming. So, two years later, in the depth of winter, she goes to visit her parents again, and ends up at the same house. Again the man comes to her and they make love, but on both nights this time. Again she seems to be in some strange kind of dreamlike state while it's going on, but she knows it's true because she sees the marks of his hands on her body the next day.'

'Anna gets pregnant again, and this time she has a son.' Nell took over. 'She becomes desperate to find her lover and when her husband goes away on business she goes to the house to find him. But the house is closed up and empty, and no one can tell her whom it belongs to. She thinks that she's lost him and is terribly sad, but when she passes that way the next winter she calls there out of sentimentality, and to her joy finds everything the way she first remembered: the same servants, the place warm and inviting, the same bed...'

'And the same lover,' Ben finished for her. 'She begins to suspect that perhaps her food or drink was drugged before, so has nothing. She leaves the lights burning in the room, wanting to see her lover's face, but it's a big old-fashioned four-poster bed with heavy curtains all round, he blows out the candles and she doesn't see him. She tries to talk to him, though, but he silences her with kisses, exhausts her with love, and when she wakes he's gone. Afraid that by trying to see him she might have lost him, that night she drinks and eats, and again it's like a dream when he comes to her.

'So every winter she goes back. She has two more children but one of them dies. She is distraught and her husband can give her no comfort. It's summer, but she goes to the house anyway, finds it empty as before. She sleeps on the bed and this time feels the warmth of his arms, his strength and love and is comforted for her loss. She leaves a locket behind with a picture of her dead child in it.'

Nell, unable just to sit and listen, took up the story again. 'Anna has a child to take the place of the one she lost, again by her lover. Twelve years have passed. Then her husband is killed in an accident, and although she's sad for him she's filled with happiness at her freedom, because now she'll be able to go and find her lover, be with him always.' She paused, her face becoming sad. 'Then her husband's possessions that he was carrying when he was killed are sent to her—and she finds the locket. And she knows the truth, and knows that she has lost not only her lover, but all the years of happiness together if she had only know the truth before.'

'I don't agree there,' Ben said matter-of-factly, breaking in on her sad sentimentality. 'If she'd realised the first time who he was, it would have been a coupling just like all the others before, and she'd never have thought that she had a phantom lover. It was the secretiveness of the affair that aroused and fed her sensuality. She'd have gone on being lonely and unfulfilled—unless she'd been driven to have an affair with the stable-boy or some other available man.' He grinned at Nell's indignant look. 'Lots of women were driven to that in those days, you know; either that or turning to religion and doing good works whether the poor liked it or not.'

'That's hypothetical,' Nell pointed out. 'The story finishes with her finding out it was her husband all along and being sad; we don't have to worry about what might have been.'

'How logical.' Ben looked round. 'Did Max say there were the tools for making coffee somewhere?'

'Yes, he did,' Nell answered, but didn't get up to look.

Ben glanced at her and grinned. He went over to the cupboard, found a kettle and cups, packets of coffee, sugar and powdered milk. 'All we appear to be short of is water,' he remarked. 'Where do we get that, I wonder?'

Satisfied she'd made her point, Nell stood up. 'I noticed a cloakroom just along the corridor; I'll get some from there.'

'Thanks.'

But the water in the cloakroom wasn't suitable for drinking and she was directed to another place on the next floor. It was almost ten minutes before she came back, and Ben was sitting on the settee, the phone in his hand, his feet up on the arm. The light from the window was behind him, outlining his profile, and for the first time Nell noticed its hardness, the leanness of his jawline and the good bone-structure. He could, she supposed, be considered good-looking, attractive to women, and wondered why she hadn't noticed before. Because she'd been too tense, probably, too worried about having to work with him, and what he would want to do with her precious story. The latter was still undecided, perhaps still to be fought over, but she felt more relaxed with him now, more able to think of him as a man.

'But surely you can manage,' he was saying. 'It's only for a few days.' He listened, then gave a resigned sigh. 'OK, OK, I'll get back as soon as I can and we'll talk it over then. Yes, I do understand. Yes. Goodbye.'

Nell had been busying herself with the coffee, but looked round to say, 'Milk and sugar?'

'What?' Ben had been gazing moodily out of the window. 'Oh—one sugar, no milk.'

She handed him a cup. 'I take milk and sugar,' she told him. He frowned, not with it. 'So you'll know when it's your turn to make the coffee,' she supplied.

His mouth crooked a little but there was obviously something else on his mind. 'I'll try and remember.'

Sitting down at the table again, she stirred her coffee and said, 'I think the first episode ought to end after her first night with her lover.'

'Sounds right.' But Ben was still frowning abstractedly. He took a swallow of the coffee but then put down the mug and stood up, his hands thrust into his pockets. He took a couple of paces round the room, head bent, then turned to frown out of the window again.

'Hasn't your crisis resolved itself?' Nell asked sympathetically.

'My what?'

'You said you were late because of a domestic crisis,' she reminded him.

'Oh—yes. I mean, no, it hasn't resolved itself.' His face changed, grew bleak, the lines at the corners of his mouth deepening and becoming bitter. 'Sometimes I don't think it ever will.' Before Nell could say anything, he glanced at his watch, picked up his briefcase, and said, 'Look, I'm sorry, but I'm going to have to leave. Why don't you make a start and I'll catch up with you tomorrow?'

'But you can't just...' Nell's voice tailed off as the door swung shut behind him.

CHAPTER TWO

NELL had wanted to do the book adaptation herself, but, perversely, when Ben abandoned her to it before they'd even got started she became indignant and angry. The word processor was pounded rather hard the rest of that day and quite a lot of work got done.

She expected him to be late again the next morning and was both surprised and irritated to find Ben there before her. Not only there but sitting at her desk and going through the work she'd done the previous day. 'My, my, aren't you the early bird,' she greeted him sarcastically, dumping her bag on the desk.

Ben glanced at her. 'Talking of birds; are you an owl or a lark?'

'What do you mean?'

'Are you up with the lark in the morning or a night owl who never wants to go to bed? A morning person or a night person?'

Nell thought about it. 'A night owl, I suppose.'

'That would account for it, then.'

'For what?'

'For your bad temper,' he said evenly.

She hung her jacket on a peg. 'I think I'm entitled to be annoyed after the way you took off yesterday. You'd only been here a couple of hours and we hadn't even got started on the book.'

'For which I apologised and came in early today,' he pointed out.

But Nell had met that male trick of trying to put you in the wrong and make you feel guilty before. 'It was extremely unprofessional,' she said shortly.

'I'm a writer, not a clock-watching clerk,' Ben told her, his voice hardening.

'Yes, but you're still a *professional* writer. You are getting paid, aren't you?'

She had expected that to needle him, but to her surprise he grinned, and said in a schoolboy voice, 'I'm very sorry, miss. I'll try to do better in future, miss.'

The grin, and the mimicry, were captivating. Despite herself, Nell smiled in return.

'That's better. I was beginning to think I'd got to work with a dragon.' That took her aback a little, but before she had a chance to say anything Ben tapped the screen with his finger. 'What you did yesterday was good, but you've written it for the ear and not enough for the eye.'

'I tried to write it visually,' Nell said defensively. 'I've read books on writing for television and studied other scripts.'

'Yes, and you've had a good shot at it, but you haven't gone into enough detail. You have to see and describe every emotion, almost every gesture. And you have to allow the time it will take the actors to show the emotions, make the gestures.'

Nell pulled up a chair and sat down beside him. 'Show me.'

His mouth crooked a little at the command in her voice, but he went back to the beginning of her script and began to go through it with her. By the end of an hour Nell was realising there was far more to television script-writing than she'd ever imagined.

'I think it would probably be best if we wrote the script as you did it yesterday and then went through each scene together putting in the camera and actors' instructions,' Ben suggested. He sat back and ran a weary hand over his eyes. 'How about a coffee?'

She didn't argue this time but got up to make it, taking some packages from her holdall-type bag. 'I brought some biscuits. Would you like one?' She opened a tin and offered it to him.

Ben raised his eyebrows. 'They look home-made,' he remarked, taking one.

'Yes, they are.'

'By you?'

She nodded.

'It's good. The coffee tastes different, too.'

'I bought some decaffeinated. And a carton of real milk. I don't like that powdered stuff.'

'You sound like a girl who likes her creature comforts,' Ben remarked.

'Of course. Don't you?'

'Oh, sure—when I can get them.' For a moment the bleak look was back in his face, but then was gone as he said, 'Are you married, Nell?'

'No. Career-girl.'

'Does that mean you live alone?'

'Yes.'

'And you actually bother to cook for yourself?'

'Yes, why not?'

'Most people who live alone seem to exist on frozen ready-made meals. From the supermarket to the freezer to the microwave. There doesn't seem to be much point in doing the shopping, spending so much time in preparation, and creating so much washing-up just for oneself.'

'You seemed to stress the washing-up,' Nell smiled.

'I don't like it, I admit,' Ben grimaced. 'But you must enjoy cooking. How did you learn?'

'My mother taught me,' Nell replied, her face and voice calm, betraying none of the inner swirl of emotions that memories of her mother always aroused. Yes, she taught me to cook, she thought bitterly. Just as she taught me to be clean and tidy, and punctual, and polite, and deferential, and come straight home, and not to make friends or talk to boys, and to be obedient, always obedient. And——

'You're lucky, my mother didn't teach me a thing,' Ben said, breaking into her thoughts, for which she was grateful. 'I never even had to boil an egg before I went to university. And the first one I tried was so rock-hard I gave up and ate out the whole time.'

'And now you exist on ready-made meals?'

'Most of the time.'

'So you're not married, either?' It was safe and acceptable to ask that because he'd asked her first.

'No.' His face hardened. 'No, I'm not.' He swung his chair round towards her. 'Do you think I could possibly have another of those biscuits? They're delicious.'

Nell grinned. 'It isn't necessary to flatter. I'll leave the tin here so just help yourself.'

They got to work again but broke off for lunch at one. Nell went out to get some fresh air and investigate the local shops, but Ben picked up the phone to call his agent, to talk over more work he'd been offered, she supposed, feeling envious of his success. When she came back he was lying on the settee, his feet up on the arm again, but this time he was asleep.

He didn't waken when she came in. Nell quietly put down the bag of shopping she'd bought, and stepped silently over towards him. She was about to reach out

and waken him, but hesitated and withdrew her arm.
He looked to be deeply asleep, and must have been very
tired. Another night on the tiles? Nell wondered. She
wouldn't be at all surprised. Most of the bachelors she
knew seemed to go out somewhere every night, living it
up, dating girls, making the most of their youth and
vitality, many of them often sweating away in gyms to
be fit enough to go out drinking, or make love to the
latest girlfriend through the night, or both.

Ben didn't look particularly dissipated, she thought,
gazing down at him. His skin was still tight around his
jawline and there was no flabbiness about his tall frame.
Muscle, yes. And a broadness of shoulder that suggested strength, but his stomach was flat, his waist lean.
Maybe he worked out regularly. Maybe he went out with
just one woman. Nell didn't think he could be living
with a woman, though, or else he wouldn't be so tired,
and he would have been looked after better; there was
a button missing from his shirt, she noticed.

It felt odd to look down at a man asleep like this. It
wasn't something she could ever remember doing before.
A man was, she supposed, vulnerable in his sleep, mo-
mentarily within one's power. But Ben didn't look very
vulnerable; his features were still hard, the lines around
his mouth still deep, even though his lashes brushed his
cheeks in a soft curve and a lock of dark hair fell forward
on to his forehead. An ambulance went by in the street
below, its siren wailing, the noise penetrating his sleep,
making him stir. Nell moved quickly away and appeared
to be just hanging up her jacket when he yawned and
sat up.

'Must have dropped off,' he murmured. 'Excuse me.'

He went out and she noticed an empty sandwich pack
and a beer can beside the settee. Fastidiously, unable to

help herself, Nell picked them up and dropped them in the waste basket. Whoever had the misfortune to end up with Ben, she thought, would have to be willing to spend her life clearing up after him, because he certainly hadn't been brought up to do it himself. For a moment she felt a fierce stab of envy, not for this imaginary woman, but for Ben's joyous disregard of the rule of neatness, his ability to go through life in blissful untidiness, either not caring or with some wretched female to do it for him. The fault of a doting mother, she supposed, and devoutly wished she'd had one who'd cared half as much.

When Ben came back his hair was damp, as if he'd thrown water over his face to wake himself up.

'You never said what you were,' she reminded him. 'A lark or an owl?'

He laughed. 'Originally a lark, but lately I've had to be an owl.'

They worked well that afternoon, except for two longish phone calls for Ben. Nell tried not to listen but couldn't avoid it. They were evidently from his agent, about the new project he was negotiating, and Ben seemed to be pushing for special working conditions. 'You know my problem,' she heard him say. 'I either work at home or in London. If they can't agree to that then tell them to get someone else.' The agent must have become exasperated, because Ben went on, 'Yes, I know it's a great opportunity, but there's no way I'm going to America... OK, see what they say and get back to me.'

Putting down the phone, he came back to where they'd been talking through a scene at the table, pads and pencils before them. 'Sorry about that,' Ben said shortly.

'That's OK.' Nell glanced at him, wondering how far she could question him. She tried an oblique approach. 'How long do you think it will take us to write the serial?'

'Depends how much re-writing Max wants done. If he's happy, then about six or seven weeks, I should think.'

'That's what I thought. I hope you'll be free for that length of time.'

'Don't worry,' Ben said drily, looking at her, knowing she'd listened. 'I promised to do this book—and I always keep my promises.'

'Oh, good.' She was strangely over-pleased. For the book's sake, she thought, but knew it wasn't. Because I'm learning a lot from him, then, and he doesn't seem to mind teaching me. Yes, that must be it, she told herself.

Ben left at three-thirty, which she thought was rather early, but then he had come in early this morning, she remembered. Maybe he'd decided those were the hours that suited him best. There didn't seem to be any point in staying on herself, so after she'd printed off the work they'd done that day she went to have a chat with Max, to reassure him that they were getting on marvellously, and to pick up any gossip that was going. Most gossip was, of course, gathered in the ladies' room, but no one that Nell knew came in, so eventually she gave up and went home.

As she cooked her solitary meal she remembered what Ben had said about frozen dinners and felt sorry for him. Maybe, she thought, the ladle in her hand forgotten as she gazed into space, I'll give a dinner party.

Ben rang in to say that he had to go to a meeting the next morning and it was almost lunchtime before he arrived. Nell had been getting on with the script, but doing it the way he'd suggested, so that they could go through the cast and camera instructions together. As she wrote she found herself becoming ever more bound up in the storyline, and closely involved with Anna as she became disillusioned with the man she'd been made to marry against her wishes. The man had seemed so aloof, so strange, what he did to her in bed so humiliating. Nell was troubled about having to write that scene. But although it was in the book, she thought it would be better just to show Anna's fear before the wedding night and then her reaction of loathing towards her husband the next morning.

She wrote the scene on those lines, but when Ben came in and read through the print-out he disagreed with her. 'You'll have to show more than that,' he told her.

'I don't see why. Explicit sex scenes are old hat nowadays. People have got bored to death with writhing bodies all over the place.' She spoke forcefully, a frown between her level brows.

Ben gave her a surprised look. 'What have you got against sex?'

Nell flushed. 'Nothing, of course,' she said quickly. 'I just think that the public are tired of having it thrust at them the whole time.'

His eyes rested thoughtfully on her face for a moment, but then Ben said, 'You don't have to be explicit. But the viewers don't expect to have the bedroom door shut in their faces any more. And don't forget we have to show the difference between the love scenes with her husband and with her lover. How the former are cold and businesslike and the latter magically sexual and satisfying.'

'Surely the actors will do that.'

'Yes, but we're the ones who are playing God; the actors will only do what we decide they will do. It's up to us to tell them what lines to say, what moves to make, how far to go.' He paused, but when she didn't speak he said, 'I really think we have to put that scene in, Nell.'

She gave a tight smile. 'You're right, of course. How do you think it should go?'

'Well, there we have the advantage of using camera angles. We could shoot it, perhaps, just watching Anna's face. We may not need any dialogue. The important thing is to show how distasteful and humiliating she finds it in comparison with her dream lover.'

Nell voiced a point that had been worrying her. 'I don't see how we're going to do that if the scenes with the lover are in the darkness of a curtained four-poster. And how are we going to avoid showing his face? If we do it will spoil the ending.'

Ben put his elbows on the table and rested his chin on his fists as he thought about it. 'There are always ways to get round problems like that. Maybe we could give the lover a mask. That would cut out problems about Anna being drugged in future scenes. That part has always worried me.'

'But he didn't wear a mask,' Nell objected.

'Nell, when you're adapting something from the printed page you have to have scope for alteration to a different medium. In a book the author can describe the characters' thought processes, go into minute detail about their feelings and emotions. Sometimes they take a whole page just to describe one kiss! You can't do that on television. There's no narrator. You have to try and show everything through the actors' words and actions. Here we have the basic problem of not being able to film in the dark, so we have to use a ploy to get round it. And giving the lover a mask would seem to be the obvious way. Don't you agree?'

'From a convenience point of view, yes, but that first night...surely he wouldn't have worn a mask the first time?'

'No, but we can get round that by making her feel cold in bed and taking a drink or two to warm her up, so that she feels woozy and isn't with it enough to get alarmed when he slips into bed and starts making love to her.'

'And then she realises that she likes what's happening to her. Yes, I suppose that could work.'

'We could have Anna saying, "Who are you?" Maybe she struggles a little, but then her body takes over before her husband can speak and identify himself. But perhaps, when it's over, she says it again.'

'If he was going to tell her who he was, that would surely have been the time,' Nell pointed out. 'Why didn't he tell her then?'

'Maybe he realised to have told her would have spoilt it all; maybe she just fell asleep,' Ben suggested. 'But we don't really have to worry about why the lover did or didn't do anything. That's all left to the imagination of the viewer.'

'Yes, I suppose so. But it has to be believable.'

'It will be.' Reaching out, he put a reassuring hand over hers, gave it a slight squeeze. 'Don't worry. We'll make your "dream" come alive.'

Bearing in mind the title of the book they were adapting, it was a good play on words. Nell smiled appreciatively. And she liked the way he had reassured her of his own accord; it showed that they were working well together, she thought, and for once she didn't mind being physically touched. 'Well, it's nice to have one dream come true,' she remarked.

Ben cocked an eyebrow at her. 'Does that mean you have other dreams?'

'Of course,' Nell answered lightly. 'Doesn't everyone? Don't you?'

'What are your dreams, Nell?'

She shrugged slightly. 'The same as every other girl's, I suppose.'

'To get married and live happily ever after?' Ben suggested wryly.

'Good heavens, no! To make a success of my career, of course.'

He burst out laughing. 'Don't tell me that's the ambition of every single girl, because I don't believe it.'

Nell smiled, pleased that she'd made him laugh. 'Well, it happens to be mine and that of most of my friends.'

'Until the right man comes along.'

'Or the wrong one,' she said pensively, then quickly said, 'How about you; don't you have any dreams?'

The sun was shining brightly through the window. Ben got up, pulled up the blind, and would have opened the window, except that it was a modern air-conditioned building and the windows wouldn't open. He banged an annoyed fist against the frame. 'I feel like a caged animal in here.' He turned, gave her a moody look as she sat waiting for him to answer. 'No,' he said harshly, 'I don't have dreams any more—just nightmares.'

Nell blinked, taken aback, but was even more surprised when Ben said, 'Come on, let's get out of here.'

Picking up a microcassette recorder, he headed for the door. Grabbing her bag, Nell followed at a run.

'Where are we going?'

'Just out. Anywhere. I'm fed up with being cooped up inside. I need to stretch my legs.'

Considering how long his legs were, Nell wasn't surprised. When they got out of the building he turned left and strode along the pavement at a brisk pace. Nell grabbed his arm. 'Hey, slow down. I can't keep up with you.'

He glanced down at her. 'Oh, sorry. You're awfully short, aren't you?'

'No,' Nell answered, annoyed. 'You're awfully tall.'

He grinned at that, and took her arm to propel her more than help her across the road.

It was one of the best things about London that there was always a park or open space somewhere near by. They had only walked for a few minutes before they turned in the gates of one, the trees and lawns making a green oasis in the heart of the city. Ben's pace immediately slowed, as if the tension had suddenly gone out of him. 'I was wrong,' he said. 'There is one ambition—dream, if you like—that I have: to own a house in the country, a place with a garden that isn't overlooked.'

'An old thatched cottage with roses round the door?'

He grinned. 'Trust a woman to think of the house first. I hadn't given it a thought; all I've imagined is the garden and being out in the open instead of stuck over a word processor. I envy the old writers who could work anywhere, or someone like George Bernard Shaw with his garden house.'

'Are the machines our slaves or are we the slaves of the machines?'

'Quite.' Ben smiled again and turned to look at her. 'I'm not used to walking with someone as short as you.'

So how was she supposed to take that? Nell wondered. Wryly she said, 'I suppose all your girlfriends are tall and willowy. Very fashionable.'

'Is it? I should have thought it was a great advantage to be short. All the tall girls have to find taller men, whereas short girls can choose from the whole range.'

'There is that, I suppose,' she admitted. 'But I'm not *that* short.'

Ben took the cassette recorder from his pocket and held it ready. 'Now, that scene we were discussing...'

Soon they were absorbed in the adaptation, but not so deeply that Nell didn't notice how pleasant it was to work like this, to breathe in the fresh air and feel a slight breeze in her hair, to walk from shade into sunlight, to smell the flowers in the beds and to hear the birds singing happily on this summer afternoon. It was easier out here, too, to discuss the wedding-night scene and how it should be handled. Anyone passing by, though, might have been startled to overhear their conversation as Ben said, 'The whole sex act shouldn't take longer than a couple of minutes,' and Nell added,

'No, and they should both have their nightclothes on the whole time.'

They sat on a seat while Ben dictated into the recorder and made good progress. But at three-thirty he glanced at his watch. 'We'd better be getting back so I can collect my car. I have to do some shopping on the way home.'

'More ready-made meals?' Nell said with a smile, creating the opportunity she wanted.

'That's right.'

She hesitated for just a moment, wondering if she wasn't being too precipitate, but then said casually, 'I'm having a dinner party on Saturday night. If you'd like

to sample some home cooking, you'd be very welcome
to come and join us.'

Ben had been walking unhurriedly along, his arms
loose at his sides, but now she felt him tense and saw
him put his hands into his pockets. Damn! she thought
angrily. He thinks I'm making a pass.

There were a couple of women pushing baby-buggies
coming towards them. Ben moved to walk round the
other side of them, giving him, she realised, time to
compose a tactful answer. He smiled at her and said,
'That's very kind of you, Nell. I'd certainly be grateful
for a good meal, but I'm afraid I'm going away this
weekend. But ask me again, will you?'

'Of course,' she said with a polite smile. 'I'll let you
know next time I have another dinner party.'

So that was that, she thought, feeling hurt. He obviously didn't want to know, even though he'd been very
polite and tactful about it. But so what? She'd only felt
sorry for the guy. It was his loss, not hers. She would
still have the dinner party; she usually gave one a month
anyway, but she had brought it forward in the hope that
Ben would come. When they reached the office he picked
up his briefcase, said goodbye, and left in a hurry.

Nell sighed. She'd made her invitation as casual as
possible, stressed that there would be other people there,
but she had obviously scared Ben off. Going to the
window, she watched as he drove out of the underground car park. He drove an ordinary estate car, which
surprised her; she'd expected him to own something more
sporty and powerful. Maybe he really was going away
for the weekend, she thought. Or perhaps he already
had a steady relationship and didn't feel free to accept
invitations from other girls. I suppose I should have
asked him to bring a friend, she mused, and then laughed

at herself. She wasn't interested in Ben's friends, wasn't even sure that she wanted to be interested in him.

They worked together amicably enough for the rest of the week, but on Friday she did some shopping in the lunch-hour, letting him know that the dinner party was going ahead. The wedding-night scene was finished to their satisfaction, although Nell had strongly disliked having to read through the dialogue aloud, to make sure it 'felt right', as Ben put it.

'I'm not an actress,' she protested. 'And, anyway, it sounds OK to me.'

'Written dialogue often sounds stilted when it's spoken. I always like to go through it aloud. And that way, too, you can get more idea of how long the scene will take.'

'What do you do when you're working alone?' Nell asked.

'Then I have to run through all the parts myself.'

'Do that now, then, and I'll listen and make any criticism I think necessary.'

Ben raised an eyebrow. 'What have you got against reading it yourself? Don't tell me you're shy.'

'No, of course not,' Nell snapped back. 'But I'm no good at that kind of thing; it will sound all wrong.'

'Let's just try it, shall we?' he said on a patient note.

Nell flashed him a look, wondering why, when she'd so openly said that she didn't want to do it, he should still expect to have his own way—and get it, too! Picking up the script, she started to read through the heroine's lines, doing so in a clipped, short tone that lacked any emotion whatsoever.

'Hey! Stop!' Ben commanded. 'What's the matter with you? Put some feeling into it.'

'I am.'

'But you're not. Look, like this.' Standing up, he read through some of the husband's lines. He had a good voice, quite deep, and was able to put almost as much emotion into it as an actor. 'Now try,' he instructed her.

Nell began to speak the lines again, and this time, almost against her will, she made them sound more realistic. Enough to satisfy him anyway. But it was so obvious that she didn't like doing it that when they'd finished Ben said to her, 'Aren't you happy with that scene?'

'Yes, it's fine.'

'You don't behave as if you are.'

She looked away. 'I told you; the scene is fine. Let's get on, shall we?'

But he gave her an assessing look and said, 'Maybe it's the sex without love part of it you don't like. But many of those arranged marriages started off with the woman submitting out of duty.'

'Lie back and think of England,' Nell said.

'That kind of thing. I suppose as a romantic you think that's all wrong?'

'What makes you think I'm a romantic?' Nell asked, immediately intrigued.

'You chose this book,' Ben replied with an expressive gesture.

'Only because I thought it would make good television. I'm not at all romantic.'

'Of course you are. All women are romantic at heart. I haven't met one yet who wasn't.'

'Well, you have now,' Nell said firmly. 'I'm a realist.'

Ben laughed, amusement in his grey eyes. He hadn't looked so tired the last couple of days and she guessed that his domestic problem, whatever it had been, must have sorted itself out. She wondered what it was; he didn't talk about his private life, hadn't opened up much at all, really.

'Don't you believe me?' she asked.

'How old are you?'

The question surprised her; she didn't know where it was leading. 'Twenty-five,' she answered warily. 'Why?'

'Then you're much too young to be a realist.'

'Why so? Do you think realism only comes with age?'

'More with experience.'

It was a risky question, but she said, 'What makes you think I'm not experienced?'

'Have you ever been married?'

'No.'

'Had a steady relationship with a man?'

Her wariness increased. 'What's that got to do with it?'

'Until you've got love, or the hope for love, safely tucked away in experience, then you've no hope of becoming a realist.'

Nell thought about that for a moment, but it brought back pictures from the past, and she said quickly, 'How about you? Would you call yourself a realist?'

A brooding look came into Ben's face. 'I suppose I am—not that I particularly want to be.'

He didn't enlarge on that remark, so Nell said, 'Are you a realist because you've got love and romance out of your system?'

His mouth hardened. 'There are other ways, ways that force you into becoming what you don't want to be.'

'What do you mean?'

But Ben picked up the script again. 'Time's getting on; let's go through this once more.'

So he ducked the question and she didn't find out anything more about him.

On Saturday Nell had her dinner party. There was only room for eight people at the gatelegged table that she placed in the middle of her sitting-room, the rest of the furniture pushed against the walls out of the way. She had several girlfriends that she'd made during the last few years, and she usually invited one of these along— with her latest boyfriend if the friend couldn't be prised apart from him for an evening, and also people she'd met through her work. As these were mostly connected with show business in some way, sometimes a quite remote way, and because the food she gave was always good and the wine plentiful, she had no worries about her invitations being accepted. Show business people were always eager to make new contacts and, in their turn, were generous in imparting any rumours they'd heard.

Occasionally Nell would have a hen-party, which she really enjoyed because the girls weren't out to make an impression and could all let their hair down, but usually, as tonight, she mixed the sexes in equal numbers. One man had found himself asked at the last minute, to take the place she'd intended for Ben, but he was glad enough to be invited not to mind. The party went well, as it always did; Nell was experienced enough now to have got the format exactly right, but somehow she didn't get as much enjoyment from it as she usually did. She felt strangely like an outsider looking on, not part of the party at all.

I must be having an off-day, she thought, and firmly rejected an up-and-coming actor's offer to help her wash up—a euphemism for spending the night with her.

Sunday she worked on the outline for a radio programme for blind children. It was an educational programme, describing the background for books they

would have to study for their O level exams. Nell had
heard about the idea through a friend in local radio and
had already talked to the producer and been asked to
submit an example, showing the way she would handle
it. The producer had warned her that there wouldn't be
a great deal of money in it, but Nell wasn't worried about
that. If her work was accepted it would be another credit
to add to her growing list, and the work would be good
practice. And, although she had to live, she wasn't so
hard up that she couldn't forgo some time and money
to help handicapped children. Helping at a distance was
better, anyway. Nell had strong feelings of guilt where
children were concerned and tended to avoid them as
much as possible.

On Monday Ben was early again. Nell hadn't expected him to be and, instead of taking the quicker
Underground, had caught a bus and then walked the
rest of the way because it was such a beautiful day. She
felt good, enjoying the sun, wearing a sleeveless summer
dress for the first time that year. The spring had been
wet and long, but now summer seemed as if it had really
arrived at last and, what was more, was determined to
make up for all the earlier bad weather by being really
hot.

Usually Nell was keen to start work, but today she
lingered, reluctant to go and shut herself away in front
of a machine. Knowing that Ben liked to be outdoors,
she was surprised to find him already in the office.

'Hello. I didn't think you'd be here yet.'

Ben glanced round, paused as he looked her over.
'Good morning. You look very feminine.'

'I always look feminine.'

'*Especially* feminine,' he said with a smile.

'I unearthed some summer clothes from the back of the wardrobe.' She came to stand beside him. 'What part are you working on?'

'The scene where Anna's mother comes to visit and tries to find out why she isn't pregnant yet.'

'Should we include in that scene the mother inviting them to stay for Christmas?'

'Yes, I think so.' Ben sniffed, and, picking up her hand, turned her wrist over and held it near his face. 'That is the most delightful scent.'

'Thank you.' She was surprised and pleased; he hadn't made any personal comment before, nor had he touched her very much.

And she was pleased again when, at around midday, he stood up and said, 'Come on, let's go out to lunch. My treat.'

She quite expected him to take her to the nearest pub, but instead he hailed a taxi and directed the driver to a restaurant with a terrace that overlooked the Thames. Her eyes widened when he ordered champagne. 'Are we celebrating?'

'Could be. I've been asked to write the screenplay for a film.'

Remembering the telephone call she'd overheard, Nell said, 'Congratulations. A British film?'

'No, American. But I've persuaded them to let me write it here rather than in Hollywood.'

'Don't you like America?'

'Of course. It's a great place, but I can't leave here at the moment.' He smiled at her. 'We have *A Midwinter Night's Dream* to finish.'

'Wouldn't they wait until we've finished it?' Nell asked, stunned that he should think it important enough to risk losing the film contract.

'Oh, yes. But I have other things that keep me here.'
A remark that put things back in perspective. The champagne came, their glasses were filled and Ben raised his in a toast. 'To our collaboration.'

'I'll drink to that. Mm, it's good. Is this how you usually live—alfresco lunches and champagne?'

'Only on the first day of summer, when I have a pretty girl to take out.'

'I'm flattered.'

His eyes met hers, warm and smiling. 'You have no need to be.'

Nell caught her breath, a little taken aback. She was far from unused to receiving compliments, and had become not just blasé about them but at times almost resented them. So many men seemed to think that compliments were necessary to sweeten a girl up, that they only had to throw out one or two and the girl would be so grateful she'd do anything they wanted. Like patting a dog on the head so it would grovel at your feet. Other men paid compliments condescendingly, the stock phrases issuing from their mouths in exactly the same way, no matter which woman they were with. And the compliments weren't really for the woman at all, but to boost her image in the man's eyes, to make her conquest the more special.

Searching Ben's face, Nell wondered in which category his compliment should be placed, but he had picked up the menu and was studying it, and made no attempt to follow it up. Which rather intrigued her. He was, she thought, rather an intriguing man altogether. But at least he seemed to be opening up a little today.

Their food ordered, Ben leaned back in his seat, making Nell say, 'You seem very relaxed today.'

'Don't I always?'

'No. Most of the time you seem to be pausing at the office before rushing off somewhere else.'

He gave a rueful grin. 'Life does seem to get like that sometimes. But thankfully I hope to be able to spend more time working on the adaptation for the next few weeks. Until we've finished it with any luck.'

'And then you'll start on the film?'

'No, I'll probably start doing an outline for it at once.'

'You're going to work on two writing jobs at the same time?' Nell asked in surprise.

Ben shrugged. 'I have to work while I have the chance.'

She thought he meant that he took all the work that was offered to him, but before she had the opportunity to ask him their food came, and then he changed the subject by saying, 'How did your dinner party go?'

'Very well.' Despite herself her voice was a little cool. 'How was your weekend?'

'OK. I went up to my parents' place.'

'Oh. Where do they live?' she asked, feeling pleased that he'd bothered to explain.

'Shropshire. How about yours?'

'My parents? Oh, they live on the south coast.'

'Do you go down there much?'

'No. This food is delicious. How did you find this place?'

'Ouch!' He put a hand up to his face.

'What's the matter?' Nell asked in surprise.

'You just slammed a door in my face.'

She flushed a little. 'Parents are boring.'

'All right; tell me about yourself, then.'

'That's even more boring.'

'Do I hear the clang of another door?'

Nell laughed, amused by him even though she didn't like the way the conversation was heading. 'There's nothing much to tell,' she said lightly. 'I wasn't brilliant at school, just had a good imagination and could write stories. So I went on a creative writing course and have been doing freelance work ever since. You know about my work, we talked about it before.'

'A very few words to sum up a life,' Ben said lightly. But his eyes were holding hers and she had the strangest feeling that he could see into her mind, read there the terrible thing that she couldn't tell anyone about.

'What about you?' she challenged.

'School. University. Hey, you'll never believe some of the things that happened there.'

He began to tell her anecdotes about college life, telling them well and making her laugh, until it was time to go back to work. Nell was entertained and amused, but she learnt little more about Ben than he had learnt about her.

But that week, while the sun shone, they got into the habit of going out together every day for lunch. Not always to a restaurant; sometimes they bought sandwiches and took them to the park, sitting on a wooden bench or, when those were full, on Ben's jacket spread out on the grass. Mostly they talked about the book, unable to put it out of their minds, but gradually they became more relaxed, found that they shared a quirky sense of humour, and were at ease with one another. Nell began to find a zest for life that she hadn't felt for a long time. She took more than usual care with her clothes and appearance, was eager to get to the office, not only to work on the book, but to see Ben as well.

He wouldn't let her pay when they went out to lunch and when she protested he said lightly, 'It's in return for all those delicious biscuits you make—and of course for that dinner party you're going to invite me to.'

Nell turned to look at him, tilting her head. 'I only have dinner parties once a month.'

'Does it have to be a party?' He was looking into her eyes again, his left eyebrow raised quizzically in that habit he had.

A strange tenseness filled her chest and she could hear the beating of her heart. This is the time to draw back, she thought, but found herself saying, 'I suppose not.'

'And do we have to wait that long?'

Taking a first, tentative step, Nell said hesitatingly, 'Well, I'm not doing anything on Wednesday evening; you could come round then, if you like?'

'I like,' he said, so promptly that she laughed.

That weekend she cleaned the flat, worked out a menu, changed her mind, changed it back again. This is silly, she thought, it's only a date. But she didn't have that many dates, preferring to go out in a crowd, to entertain a crowd. There weren't that many men in the past whom she'd wanted to get to know better, none whom she'd allowed to get really close. But Ben was different, somehow. He was older, successful, self-confident. And he was a writer, like herself. That was what made him special, she thought, trying to ignore the fact that he was also masculinely good-looking and that she found him physically attractive. But she was happy and excited that weekend as she hadn't been for a long time.

But on Monday morning everything changed. He was late, and when he did finally arrive at the office he was leading a small boy by the hand. Looking at Nell, the tiredness back in his eyes, Ben said shortly, 'This is my son.'

CHAPTER THREE

NELL'S eyes widened incredulously. 'But I thought you said you weren't married!'

'I'm not—now.'

'Oh.' A great feeling of disappointment and disillusionment ran through her, despite Ben making it clear that his marriage was over. Stifling it, she looked at the boy. He seemed to be about five or six years old, a thin child with tiredness in his eyes that matched his father's. 'Why have you brought him here?'

'I don't have anyone to leave him with.' Ben dropped a fully loaded holdall on to the floor. 'I took him up to my parents' place last weekend. He was supposed to spend the whole summer there so that I could work.'

'What happened?'

Ben crossed to the kettle and plugged it in. He glanced at the boy. 'Do you want a drink, Mark?' The boy nodded and Ben fished in his pocket for some money. 'There's a drinks machine down the corridor to the left. Get yourself a Coke or something.' When he'd gone, Ben said, 'He doesn't sleep very well and he kept them awake. When he called out on Friday night my mother went to see to him and didn't notice one of his toy cars that he'd left on the floor. She trod on it, fell, and broke her wrist. So I had to go and bring him home.'

'How terrible.' Nell still felt taken aback, unable to cope with this new situation, this new Ben as a father, an ex-husband, instead of the single, unattached man she'd thought him. 'But who looked after him before?'

'He was at school during the day until the end of term.
I used to drop him off with a neighbour who took him
to school and brought him home and hung on to him
until I could get there in the afternoon. Sometimes she
couldn't make it in the mornings, though, so I had to
take him myself.'

Which explained his late arrivals and need to leave
early, Nell realised. 'It must be very difficult for you,'
she sympathised.

'For me, and for the thousands of other one-parent
families,' Ben said with a shrug.

'Couldn't your wife——?' Nell broke off as the door
opened and Mark came back.

He was carrying his can of drink, frosted from the
cold of the machine, and set it down on top of the pile
of printed script sheets Nell had just run off and put on
the table. Quickly she moved it, but it had already left
a wet ring. 'I'll get you a mug,' she said.

Ben smiled. 'Kids usually drink out of the cans nowadays. I haven't introduced you. Mark, this is Nell, who
I'm working with.'

The boy's large, fatigue-smudged eyes settled on her,
looked her over, made her feel nervous. She had been
an only child, had no experience whatsoever of children.
'Hello, Mark,' she said, feeling inadequate.

He didn't answer, just looked at her indifferently.

'She makes fantastic biscuits,' Ben said encouragingly.

'Oh—yes.' Nell rushed to get the tin and open it.
'Would you like one?'

Mark took one, looked at her gravely and said, 'Thank
you.' Then he walked over to stand by his father.

Ben was so tall that the child only came up above his
knee. Ben reached down to pat his head, somewhat ruefully, Nell thought, then led him to the settee. 'Look,

I've got to work, so you sit here and have your drink and read some of your books, OK? Then later on I'll take you out for something to eat.'

'When are we going home?' Mark asked as Ben gave him some picture books from the holdall.

'This afternoon. When I've finished my work.'

'Help yourself to some more biscuits, if you'd like some,' Nell told the boy.

He didn't answer so she just put the open tin beside him on the settee and went back to her desk. They had reached the stage in the adaptation where Anna got stranded in the snow and found the house. Where her lover came to her for the first time. It was a part that had to be dealt with carefully, had to be just right, romantic and sensual without going over the top. Nell had made a start on it and Ben came to sit beside her and read it through.

'Yes, you're on the right lines. The trouble with the book is that it's all description here; we have hardly a line of dialogue we can use. So we'll just have to use the cameras to do the description for us, which means putting in very careful camera directions. Have you ever been in a television studio?'

'Yes, but only from the front, to watch quiz shows and things. Not when a drama was being filmed.'

'In that case it will probably help you to watch a serial being made. I'll find out if there's one in production at the moment and arrange for us to watch.'

'That would be great.'

'OK. Now let's see . . .' Ben sat down at the desk and she moved aside to let him get at the keyboard. 'How about if we have him come to the bed where she's sleeping? He draws aside the curtain of the four-poster and the moonlight shines on her face. But the light is behind him so that he's nothing but a black silhouette. We see him pull back the covers to reveal the outline of her body, perhaps the nightdress unlaced to show her cleavage and the bottom pulled up to show her legs. He climbs into bed with her.'

'With his clothes on?'

'No, perhaps not. We could let him slip outside the curtain and then come back naked.'

'Really naked?' Nell asked. 'Or just the camera angle making it look that way?'

'Depends on whoever directs it. Or on Max's budget.'

'Why his budget?'

'Actors ask for more money when they have to do nude scenes.'

'Oh, I see.' Nell laughed. 'And I thought they'd do anything for artistry.'

Ben grinned. 'Now we have to show Anna coming half awake, realising what's happening, struggling a little, but then succumbing to him. Then them making love and her enjoying it, and being amazed at how wonderful it is. We can give her some lines there. We can——'

'Daddy?' A small hand pulled at him.

He broke off. 'What is it, Mark?'

The boy gave Nell a shy glance, pulled at Ben again and make him lean down, and whispered in his ear.

'You'll have to excuse us for a few minutes, Nell.'

They went out together, the tall man with the little hand held so trustingly in his. A father. A son. Nell watched them go and had a sudden, terribly strong moment of yearning for what might have been. An intense sorrow for what she'd lost. Fighting it, bludgeoning it out of her mind, she turned back to the screen, trying to force herself to concentrate. But to get back into the past of Victorian England when the past

of seven years ago was so vivid in her mind was
impossible.

When Ben and Mark came back she was standing at
the window, the blind up, looking out. She glanced towards them. 'Why don't you come and look out of the
window, Mark? Look, there's a bus going by. Have you
ever been on one of those red double-decker buses?'

He climbed on to the settee and looked out, then
glanced at Nell and shook his head.

She left him there and came over to sit beside Ben
again. 'A man of few words,' she remarked.

'He's a bit shy.'

'How old is he?'

'Six, going on seven.'

She hadn't thought the boy was as old as that. It made
her quickly look at Mark again, wondering, comparing.

'Are you OK?' Ben asked her.

'Yes, of course.' Her voice sharpened. 'Why shouldn't
I be?'

'You look a little pale, that's all.'

'No, I'm fine.'

They started to work again, but the scene they were
discussing was intimate, to say the least. Nell, glancing
at Mark, lowered her voice, which made Ben grin.

'He doesn't understand what we're talking about.'

Nell flushed a little. 'Even so, it doesn't seem right to
talk about—about adult things in front of a child.'

'Forget about him,' Ben advised. 'Just concentrate on
what we're doing.'

But that wasn't so easy now; Nell tried but found that
she couldn't lose herself in the script as she had before.
And it was made even more difficult when Mark started
running his cars along the windowsill and making the
appropriate sounds. Ben seemed to be able to cut the

noise out, but Nell couldn't. Noticing, Ben told Mark
to be quiet and read his books, but soon the little boy
came over and wanted to be taken up on his lap.

'Not now, Mark; I'm working.'

'I want to go home.'

Ben glanced at his watch. 'It's near enough lunchtime.
I'll take him out for a hamburger. Would you like to
come with us?' he offered.

Nell shook her head. 'Thanks, but I've got some
shopping to do—for Wednesday.'

'See you later, then.' He'd got to the door before Ben
remembered. 'Oh—Wednesday.' He gave her a rueful
look. 'I'm afraid I'll have to try and get a baby-sitter
now, which might not be so easy; the neighbour who
usually sits for me has gone on holiday.'

'Maybe I'd better postpone doing the shopping, then?'
Nell said lightly. 'Until you know for sure.'

'It might be best. Sorry, Nell.'

'Think nothing of it.' She smiled, hiding her disappointment, and didn't make any attempt to go with them.

When they came back after lunch Mark was tired and
grumpy. Ben tried to settle him on the settee for a sleep,
but the boy kept getting up and coming to him, wanting
attention, wanting to go home.

It was impossible to work. After an hour or so, Nell
said, 'Look, why don't you take him home? I'll finish
off this scene as best I can and then I'll fax it through
to you.'

'Maybe that would be best.' Ben put his hands up to
his neck, rubbed it. 'I'm sorry about this. I thought I'd
got everything worked out beautifully for the next few
weeks.'

They left and Nell settled down to work again, but
after a while gave up and sat down on the settee, won-

dering if Ben would have told her about his son at all
if things had worked out with his mother. It seemed
strange that he hadn't mentioned Mark or his wife
before. How long ago had they split up? she wondered.
And for what reason? And why was Ben looking after
Mark instead of the boy's mother? Had Ben's wife just
abandoned the child when she left? These and many
more questions filled her mind. All of them un-
answerable. She felt a surge of anger against this unknown wife of Ben's. How could the woman possibly
just go off and leave them, especially Mark, who——?

Nell's mind froze as she suddenly remembered that
she had no right to such virtuous indignation. Not only
did she not know the circumstances that had made Ben
and his wife split up, but she, of all people, had certainly
no moral justification in condemning another for the
very act that she herself had committed. Only it was so
long ago now, had been so determinedly pushed out of
her mind, that sometimes it seemed as if it had never
really happened, had been just a bad dream. No, not a
bad dream, the worst nightmare of her life.

Leaning her head back against the settee, the noise of
the traffic outside humming in her ears, Nell closed her
eyes, and once again let herself remember.

She had been seventeen, the only child of strict parents
to whom she had been born late in life. Her parents
hadn't wanted children, had expected never to have any,
but, although her mother had been almost too old to
bear a child, it hadn't occurred to either of them to ter-
minate the pregnancy. That would have been a crime
against nature. They would just have to make the best
of it. But when Nell was born they were already set in
their ways, especially her father, who was nearly sixty,
and they resented the intrusion she made into their staid

and peaceful lives. Physically they were middle-aged, mentally they were already old. And they made her conform to their lifestyle, making few concessions to childishness or youth.

She had been Eleanor, never Nell. She had gone to church regularly as well as to bible classes; she had been sent to a small school that taught on traditional lines, a school for girls only. She had been taken and fetched, not allowed to stay for any extra-curricular activities, or to visit friends. There had been no little tea-parties for her on her birthdays, and her presents had always been books or clothes, both the sort that her parents thought suitable and therefore unexciting and 'respectable'—a word that was always on their lips.

Longing to be with other children, Nell had begged to be allowed to join the Brownies and later the Guides, but her mother had thought them tomboyish and unnecessary. Holidays had been spent either at home, so that her father could do some redecorating of an always pristine house, or else with some of her parents' friends, taking some kind of educational course where she had felt a nuisance. But then, she had always felt a nuisance, always known that she had been a biological mistake, tolerated because that was the right thing to do. But her parents had done their duty by this cuckoo in their nest, teaching her to knit and sew, to cook and be clean and tidy, cleanliness in that household definitely being a close second to godliness.

By the time she was seventeen Nell had been ready to rebel, ripe for any chance to show her independence, and had a natural curiosity about those alien creatures—boys. A species she had seldom come in close contact with, and about whom the girls at school never seemed to stop talking. So she had been a bud ripe for the plucking when she'd lied to her parents and told them she was going to a carol concert with the school but instead had gone to a schoolfriend's birthday party. There were boys there, and they had brought wine to drink. The friend's parents had been at the house so nothing had happened there, but one of the boys had offered to walk her home.

Nell had been glad to accept his offer, because the couple of glasses of wine she'd drunk, the first in her life, had made her head feel strange. It was on the way home that he had pulled her into the garden of a big old house, into an empty garage, and had sex with her on the floor. It had hurt but he had put a hand over her mouth to stifle her cry of pain. It had all been over very quickly, so quickly that she could hardly believe it had happened. He had lain there for a while, panting, while tears of silent fear ran down her cheeks, then he'd pulled her to her feet, walked her to her gate, and said, 'See you,' and left. She hadn't even known his full name. Not then. When she'd realised, with terror, that she might be pregnant, she had tried to find him through her schoolfriend, and then gone to wait for him outside his school. When she'd told him, looking to him for advice, for help, he'd turned on her and called her such terrible names: 'slut' and 'tart'. 'You needn't think you're going to pin it on me,' he'd shouted at her. 'I'll get every boy in the school to say he's been with you, that you're just a cheap lay.'

Sick and humiliated, frightened by his violence, Nell had run home. Terrified of her parents' reaction, she had tried to keep it a secret until she could find out what she ought to do, could summon up the courage to do it. But her mother soon found out; she kept too close a watch on her not to guess almost at once.

They had moved house. It was the only way her parents could think of to keep their shame secret. No matter that the same thing had happened to thousand upon thousand of other young girls in exactly the same way; to them it was a personal disgrace, another burden she had placed on lives that she had already ruined. There had been no point in mentioning a termination; Nell knew that and was relieved by it. It had been as unthinkable to her as it had to her parents; it was the only thing in which they were in accord. When they moved she was sent to a special school to await the birth of the child. When it was born it was to be adopted. They had told her that. There was to be no choice.

Nell had been a very young seventeen, had been taught to obey unthinkingly all her life, but even so she might have rebelled, might have tried to assert her rights. But when she was eight months pregnant, on a wet September day, a car skidded and knocked into her where she was standing on the kerb, waiting for a bus. She wasn't seriously hurt, but was unconscious off and on for a few days. The child had been born prematurely, and, when she'd finally come to, her mother had told her it had died.

'Bearing in mind the car accident, it's hardly a surprise,' her mother had said when she'd begun to cry. 'It's best you just forget about it and get on with your education.'

'What was it?'

Her mother hesitated. 'What does it matter? Forget it.'

'I want to know. If you won't tell me I'll ask the nurse.'

'All right. It was a boy.' The elder woman stood up. 'Now that you're better you may as well come home and I'll look after you. They need the beds here.'

So Nell had gone home, her first pathetic attempt at rebellion having ended in misery for them all. She had gone to a new school to study for her exams, but quite by chance, when out shopping one day, had run into one of the nurses from the hospital.

The woman had smiled and stopped. 'Hello. I don't suppose you remember me. I was on duty the day they brought you into the hospital, but I went on holiday a couple of days later. I'm pleased to see you've recovered from your accident. We were all worried you might lose your baby and were so pleased he was all right. How is he now? Getting quite big, I suppose?'

'I—I don't know.' Nell had stared at her dumbly. 'I never—I haven't seen him.'

'Oh, did you give him up for adoption? Sorry, love, I didn't know. I haven't worked on that ward since. Well, I'm sure it was for the best. You're much too young to bring up a child; not much more than a child yourself.'

The woman had walked away, embarrassed, leaving Nell standing on the pavement, stunned by disbelief. Straight away she had gone and found out the truth; that the child had been born fit and well and had since been adopted, her mother having signed the necessary papers in her name.

Thinking about it, Nell knew that the nurse was right— that she was much too young to have taken on the responsibility of caring for the baby herself. Also, she was pleased that it had gone to someone who really wanted a baby. She knew what it was like to be brought up in a home where a child was only tolerated, and not shown any affection, and could neither give nor receive joy or the love of life. Better, then, that the poor little baby should be adopted, but Nell bitterly resented her parents' having taken the decision out of her hands and lied about

it. Were they really afraid that she would have brought
her child home to be brought up by *them*, after the way
they'd treated her? But it wasn't really their fault, any
more than it had been hers.

Growing up almost overnight, Nell had said nothing
about what she had learnt. She'd stayed with her parents
until her eighteenth birthday, then thanked them for
doing their duty by her, but said that she was now leaving
to make her own way in life.

They had protested enough for conformity and even
kissed her goodbye when she left, which had surprised
Nell, for they were the opposite of demonstrative. But
she couldn't help but see the relief in their eyes, their
thankfulness that the worries were over and they could
live their own, quiet, shadowy lives again. The cuckoo
had finally flown.

Taking a room in a women's hostel, Nell had carefully
built up her own life, making the friendships she'd never
had, embarking on a writing career while holding down
an ordinary job to earn a living, having failures, and
then more and more successes. She'd learnt how to spend
money wisely, how to dress, put on make-up. Learning
how to be sociable, how to be assertive, how to behave
towards men, those had been the hardest lessons to learn,
and it had been several years before she had sex with
another man.

It hadn't been a success, mainly because she'd gone
into it almost in a manner of defiance; an experiment
to find out if it could be good, if it could be worth all
the talk, all the emotion, all the trouble it aroused. And
found it wasn't. But basically Nell was an ordinary girl
with ordinary appetites; her body instinctively wanted
physical love, even though she mentally didn't think
much of it. And as for love—that emotion that made

the world go round, was a reason for living, and filled record shops and library shelves—it had never yet come her way, and she rather thought that if she saw it coming she would definitely go out of her way to avoid it.

The latter also applied to children; she avoided them as much as possible, especially babies, because they made her remember, just as she was doing now.

Nell sighed and opened her eyes. She had no reason to feel guilty about the child she had given away; she knew that it had been for the best; but there were times when guilt and remorse filled her soul, no matter how hard she tried to fight them down. Seldom, though, did she let herself think of the child that baby had grown into, wonder what it looked like, whether he was happy. But seeing Mark, learning that they were close in age, had made her imagination start to work. And that wouldn't do at all. Her son, wherever he was, was leading his own life, the life that she had given him but must never see. And she, in her turn, must get on with the life that she'd chosen for herself. And as she'd early on decided to make a success of it, she'd just better stop mooning about on this settee and get on with some work.

Going over to the desk, Nell cleared her mind of everything else and concentrated on the script. She worked for three hours solid, then took the work into another office to fax it through to Ben's home number. Tired now, she went back to their office and collected her things together. The biscuit tin was still on the end of the settee where Mark had left it. She picked it up, frowned in surprise, and took off the lid. It was completely empty; he'd eaten the lot. Nell laughed, and then, stupidly, began to cry.

* * *

The phone rang the next day when she was still doing her morning exercises. It was Ben.

'Look, I'm sorry to have to ask you, but can you come over to my place to work today? I haven't been able to find anyone to look after Mark.'

'What about all our notes and the stuff on disks? They're all at the office,' she prevaricated.

'I have the work you faxed to me yesterday; we can go through that today.'

'OK. Where do you live?'

'In Swiss Cottage.' Ben gave her the address and added, 'Take a taxi; I'll pay.'

'Certainly not. It won't take me much longer to get there than to the office.'

It was another gorgeous day. Nell put on as little as possible, looked up bus and Tube routes, and made her way to the address Ben had given her. It turned out to be the bottom flat of a house set in an Edwardian terrace of red-brick houses in a quiet, tree-lined avenue. Nice. She rang the bell and Mark opened the door to her.

'Hello.'

'Hello, Mark. How are you today?' she said brightly.

'OK.'

She went inside and he closed the door. He didn't look so tired this morning, she noticed, and there was more colour in his cheeks. He led her downstairs to the basement, where there was a big country-style kitchen with a central table and an old Welsh dresser, its shelves full of old blue and white patterned plates. Nell looked round and knew immediately that the décor had been chosen by Ben's wife; it was far too feminine to be a man's choice. So he must have lived with her here in this flat.

Ben was standing at the sink, doing the washing-up. 'Hello, Nell. Sorry to bring you out here.'

'No problem.'

She automatically reached for a teacloth to start drying the dishes, but Ben said, 'That's OK—that's Mark's job.'

'Oh, sorry. Just habit.' She gave the cloth to Mark and watched as he reached up to carefully take the wet dishes from the drainer and start to dry them. Ben was so tall and he so short. Short for his age, Nell thought, and strangely so when he was Ben's son. But perhaps he was the sort of child that would suddenly shoot up when he was in his teens.

'Would you like a coffee?' Ben asked.

'No, thanks. You got the stuff I faxed through OK, then?' she asked, for something to say.

'Yes.' Ben turned to glance at her. 'You did a lot. What time did you leave?'

She shrugged. 'I can't remember exactly. Around nine, I think.'

'This adaptation must be playing hell with your social life,' he remarked.

'My social life always comes second to work,' she answered lightly.

Pausing, Ben turned to look directly at her. 'Do you really mean that?'

'Yes, of course. Doesn't yours?'

He gave a short laugh. 'At the moment my social life is virtually non-existent. But yours shouldn't be; you must make the most of your youth, Nell. It goes by all too fast.'

'Yes, Grandpa,' she mocked.

For a moment Ben looked surprised, but then he laughed, although there was a reluctant note to it. 'That bad, was it?'

'Worse.'

A bleak look came into his eyes. 'I must be getting old.'

Nell didn't like the bleakness, wanted to change it, so she said, 'You don't look it.'

She had put no inflexion in her voice, had kept her face quite straight, but all the same Ben looked up from drying his hands, his eyes searching her face. She gave nothing away, meeting his gaze squarely—but an arrested expression now replaced the bleakness in his eyes.

'I work upstairs,' he told her, and led the way, leaving Mark to finish drying up.

His workroom was at the back of the house. A high-ceilinged room that had old-fashioned French doors leading out on to a small patio and a pocket-sized garden. There were tubs that must once have contained a lot of plants standing on the mellow York-stone of the patio, but they were now empty or neglected. The garden had a small lawn which badly needed cutting, and the flower borders round its edge were sadly overgrown.

'I see you don't like gardening,' Nell commented.

Ben looked out at the garden, almost as if he hadn't really noticed it before. 'I suppose it does need some work on it. I never seem to have the time, somehow.'

He showed her the layout of the room. He had two computers as well as a photocopier, fax, answerphone, lap-top; all the latest technology.

'Do you ever actually put pen to paper?' she asked him.

He grinned. 'It has been known.'

She moved over to look at his book collection, the shelves holding it filling an entire wall. 'I envy you this,' she said, her eyes going over the titles. 'You've got some really good reference books here.'

'They're books I've acquired over the years, as I've needed or come across them.'

'Isn't that a copy of Darwin's *The Descent of Man*?' She pointed to a book on a higher shelf, and reached up to take it down. But she wasn't tall enough and swayed a little. Ben quickly put a steadying hand on her arm, the other on her waist. For a moment she was very close to him—and very aware of it. But then she stood back and laughed. 'Thanks. I'm not tall enough for this room,' she said wryly.

He took the book down, and his hand touched hers as he handed it to her. Nell glanced at him under her lashes, was aware that he was looking at her intently, but she took the book and turned away, towards the bright sunlight that flowed in through the open windows.

'What a beautiful book. It's quite an early edition, isn't it?'

'Yes.' Ben came over to stand beside her, watched as she handled it with awed care. 'You're obviously a book-lover. By that I don't mean that you just love reading, but that you love books for what they are.'

She nodded. 'I understand. And you're right; I've always thought of books as precious things.' She gave the book back to him to return to the shelf. 'Are all these books yours?' she asked him.

'Yes, of course.' He looked surprised.

'I meant did your wife choose any of them, or are they all your own collection.'

'Oh, I see. No, they're all mine. My wife didn't read a lot.' Going over to one of the computers, he sat down. 'We'd better get started.'

They worked all morning, and both of them brought a professional, objective manner to their work, but now it somehow wasn't so easy to discuss the scene where

Anna and her lover come together for the first time. Mark had gone out into the garden to play with his toys, so it wasn't his innocent presence that held them back. Maybe it was the heat of the day that made Nell put up her bare arms to lift her hair off her neck, to kick off her shoes and put her feet, the small neat nails pink-polished, up on a stool. Maybe it was the heat as well that brought a film of sweat to Ben's brow, made him get up and pace the room to help him think. He was wearing just ragged denim shorts and a T-shirt, his legs strong and tanned.

There was no mention of coffee today; without asking, Ben brought three ice-cold cans from the fridge and Mark came to join them as they drank. 'Can we go to the swimming-pool, Dad?' he asked hopefully.

'Not this morning, Mark. Nell and I have to work. Maybe this evening.'

The boy accepted it without argument and went back into the garden.

Ben looked at her. 'We don't seem to be getting on too well, do we?'

'It's the heat.'

'I suppose so. Now where did we get to?'

He sat at the desk and Nell pulled up a chair and glanced at the monitor. 'They've made love for the first time. We've seen from her reaction how good it was. She's laughing and crying all at the same time. Can an actress really portray that, do you think?' she asked dubiously.

'If she's good enough. And I'm sure Max will make quite sure we get someone really good.'

'I hope so. He sits up, as if he's going to leave, but she catches his arm. That's as far as we've got.'

'OK.' Ben leaned back in his chair, his eyes half closed as he pictured the scene in his mind. 'Anna can put her arms round him from behind, hold him close against her bare chest. "Don't go. Please don't go," she'll beg him. His head will come up in surprise because she's never said anything like that to him before. Yes?'

'The viewers won't know that yet,' Nell pointed out. 'They'll think he's a stranger.'

'Fair enough, but we have to give him some reaction. Perhaps he can kiss her hand.'

Getting restlessly to her feet, Nell came to look over his shoulder as he typed it in. 'Mm. And then she can say, "Who are you? Tell me who you are," which must bring his head up. And surely then the light will show who he is?'

'Not necessarily. Let's try it. You do the actions we've given to Anna.'

For a moment Nell stiffened, strangely disturbed by the idea. Ben sat still, waiting, and made no move to hurry her. Licking lips gone dry, Nell slowly put her hands on his arm. '"Don't go. Please don't go,"' she read out, her voice sounding completely unnatural.

Ben sat back a little and she raised her arms to put them round him, feeling his shoulders tense beneath her hands. His head bent and she felt his lips against her hand, hot and dry. '"Who are you?"' she whispered. '"Tell me who you are."' Ben didn't raise his head, but let it, and his whole body, grow still with taut awareness.

For a moment neither of them moved, then Mark came to the window and Nell quickly straightened up and Ben sat forward. 'How do you think that will work?' he asked, his voice thick.

'Fine. The tension in his body should get the message over.'

Mark went through to another room, came back with some more toys. The child hadn't said a word, probably hadn't noticed a thing, but Nell felt oddly guilty. She became very businesslike; they both did, and managed to get more work done before Ben said it was time for lunch.

They had a salad, the three of them, sitting at a white-painted table in the garden. Then Ben got out a couple of loungers and insisted that Nell stretch out while he and Mark cleared up. When he came back he was alone.

'Where's Mark?'

'He got tired so I put him to bed for a rest. He doesn't sleep very well at night—gets nightmares.'

Nell glanced up at the other flats. 'Are you overlooked much here?'

'Usually, but the people above us are on holiday, and the couple in the top flat are both at work today. Why?'

For answer, Nell hitched up her skirt. 'I'd like to get my legs brown.'

'You need a swimsuit.'

'If I'd known you had a garden like this, I would have brought one.'

His voice sounding strange, reluctant, Ben said, 'I can lend you one, if you like.'

But she knew that it could only be one that his wife had left behind so Nell said, 'Thanks, but I won't bother.'

Ben pulled off his shirt and stretched out on the lounger beside hers. 'We'll rest for half an hour and then get back to work.'

'Fine.'

The heat was enervating, the sun and stillness a cocoon that drew Nell almost immediately into sleep. But she wasn't tired enough to go to sleep for long, and after about twenty minutes she woke feeling hot and thirsty.

Ben, too, had fallen asleep, deeply so from the look of
him. Without waking him she went inside and down into
the kitchen to get a drink. A door near the kitchen was
ajar and she could see Mark lying on top of his bed,
clutching a toy in his inert arms. It was a typical boy's
room, with spaceship wallpaper and posters, but it was
very tidy, almost unnaturally so. Also in the basement
were a cloakroom, a bathroom, a laundry-room, and a
big storeroom lined with shelves that held some bottles
of wine and a lot of sealed cardboard boxes.

Stripping off her clothes, Nell used the shower in the
bathroom to cool off, finding a towel in the cupboard
on which to dry herself. There was a full-length mirror
on the wall in which she saw that there was a pink tone
to the skin on her legs from the sun. It didn't matter;
she was fortunate in having the kind of skin that soon
went brown, but if the sun was that hot then Ben would
fry if he didn't wake soon. Luckily the big fridge was
well-stocked with bottles of beer and cans of soft drinks.
Carrying a couple of cans, Nell went back upstairs and
opened doors to rooms she hadn't yet seen. There was
a sitting-room on the left of the hall at the front of the
house, tastefully furnished but looking dusty and unused.
On the right was a large bedroom with a king-size double
bed and what looked to be a bathroom opening off it.
The bed was unmade and there were clothes lying around
in this room so Ben must use it. At the back of the house,
behind the bedroom and next to Ben's workroom, was
a much smaller room that this time looked very lived in.
It had a television set, music system, and a box of Mark's
toys. There were a couple of easy-chairs facing the television set, one of which had a pile of newspapers and
books on it, and the other the shape where someone had
sat there for long hours, Ben presumably.

He was still asleep. Nell stood between him and the sun so that his head was in shadow, wondering how to wake him. Gently or not. Not, she decided, and put one of the ice-cold cans against the bare skin of his upper arm. He woke with a start, sitting up a little and blinking at the darkness of her silhouette outlined by the sun's rays. His face became eager, his eyes brilliant, and he opened his mouth to say something, then suddenly stopped. For a second he was absolutely still, his body a tense coil, but then he visibly relaxed and his mouth crooked as he said, 'Sadist.'

Nell smiled and was about to speak, but couldn't because Ben reached up and put his hand behind her neck, pulled her down and kissed her.

It didn't start out as a passionate kiss, more one born of the sun and languidness. Unhurried, exploring, finding a mouth that felt and tasted good and wanting to know more of it. Being above him Nell had to do her share of the kissing, and, strangely for her, didn't hold back any. She liked the hardness of his lips, the soft, warm touch of his tongue, the faint muskiness of the aftershave that lingered on his skin. It was a satisfying kiss, one that opened up all kinds of new possibilities but didn't commit them to anything. Or that was what she supposed. When she thought it had gone on long enough, Nell tried to draw back, but Ben's grip on her neck tightened and he continued to hold her against his mouth. And now he took a more active part, raising his head, putting his free hand on her shoulder. His lips, too, became more importuning, more demanding as the kiss deepened. She could feel the growing tension in his body, the sweat on his skin, the hastening beat of his heart. Again she tried to break away and again he wouldn't let her. So she simply dropped both the heavy cans of drink in his lap.

'Ouch!' He let her go at once and she quickly stepped back.

'I think you need a cold drink,' she said mockingly, rescuing her own.

'I'm afraid you're right.' He swung his legs off the lounger, walked down to the end of the garden for a few minutes, then turned and came back, picked up the can and took a long drink. Nell watched his throat working, thought what a good body he had. 'Look,' he said uncomfortably, 'I'm sorry. I——'

She stood up. 'For what?' She shrugged. 'It was only a kiss. Let's get back to work, shall we? We've had much longer than half an hour.'

She went back into the workroom and after a few moments he followed her inside.

Strangely enough, they worked well together that afternoon, perhaps both of them finding it easier to concentrate on a work of fiction than on reality, both determined to put that kiss out of their minds. But Nell instinctively knew that wasn't to be the end, that Ben was fully, sexually aware of her now and had to keep a firm hold on himself not to let it show. Mark woke up and came into the room, again asking to be taken swimming, so they broke off for a while so that Ben could give him some attention. From time to time, the boy seemed to want to be near Ben, to need him to be close, which was understandable enough if his mother had walked out on him.

Ben got a story book out and they read it together, Ben helping Mark with the words he didn't understand, although to Nell's inexperienced eyes he seemed to read well for his age. She said so, and both father and son looked pleased. Mark went into the den to watch television afterwards, but they broke up about four so that Ben could take him swimming.

'Do you want to work here again tomorrow?' she asked him.

'No, I think it will be better if you go into the office tomorrow. I have to visit a couple of child-minders; see if they can take Mark when I have to go out. And I have a meeting in the afternoon about the film, so I probably won't get into the office at all. Do you mind working by yourself?'

'No, that's OK. I'll do the same as I did yesterday—work on the script as much as I can, and then we'll go through it together.' She gathered her things together and walked to the front door. 'See you Thursday, then?'

Ben seemed about to nod, but suddenly shot out a hand and gripped her arm. 'You asked me to dinner tomorrow night.'

She turned to look at him, found his grey eyes fixed intently on her face, his mouth tight. 'So?'

'Is it still on?'

'What about Mark?'

'I'll find someone to look after him. So is it still on?'

His voice was harsh, his hand tightened and she could feel the heat of it on her arm, feel the tension in his grip. And she knew that he was asking for far more than just a date. Knew, too, that if she said no then they would go on as they had, merely as collaborators for this one book. But if she said yes, then that kiss out in the garden would be the start of a much more intimate relationship.

Nell's eyes gazed into his, her lips parted as she remembered the exotic sensuality of his kiss. Then she blinked and moved away, opened the door. Ben let go of her arm, his mouth closing on his disappointment. Glancing back at him, she said, 'Seven-thirty. Number twenty-nine, Blackstock Mews.' And walked quickly away.

CHAPTER FOUR

NELL went into the office the next morning, but took the afternoon off to prepare dinner—and to prepare herself as well.

She washed her hair and gave herself a manicure, made some of her speciality boozy ice-cream and, after a moment's thought, added a couple of extra tablespoons of rum to the mixture before putting it in the freezer. Carefully sorting through her clothes, Nell chose a silver-coloured sleeveless top with a matching pair of evening trousers and carefully pressed them. She made a vegetable terrine for a starter and salmon *en croute* for the main course, with a bottle of decent wine that she put in the fridge to chill. The flat was already clean, it always was, but she gave a last dust round just before she went to have a bath and change.

As she'd expected, her skin had gone brown already, and she knew that she looked good in the silver outfit—slim, petite, pretty, her face not quite regular enough to be beautiful, her height too short for her to be considered sophisticated, but good enough. She would do.

At seven she set the table near the window at the rear of her flat, overlooking the gardens of the large houses on which the mews backed, added slender candles in tall holders and a centrepiece of flowers in a low bowl. Then she paused, wondering if she'd overdone it, whether she'd created too intimate an atmosphere than was warranted by one kiss. She took the candles away and instead inserted a fat, stumpy one in the middle of the flowers.

Most dinner guests arrived a polite ten minutes late to give the hostess time to get completely organised; Ben arrived on the dot of seven-thirty. Nell smiled to herself as she ran down to open the door, smiled wider when she saw that Ben carried a large bouquet of flowers and a bottle of wine.

'Hello, Nell.'

'Hi, come on in. What gorgeous flowers. Thank you.'

She took the flowers from him and would have turned to lead the way upstairs, but Ben put his hand on her shoulder, turned her round and kissed her lightly but deliberately on the mouth. Nell coloured slightly, recognising it for what it was—a renewal of yesterday's intimacy, a tacit statement of intent which gave her no opportunity to withdraw behind the old demarcation lines.

'I hope you found your way all right,' she said rather unsteadily as she preceded him up the stairs. 'I forgot to tell you how to get here.'

They went into her sitting-room and Ben said, 'You didn't have to; I've been here before.'

'You have?' She gave him a puzzled glance.

'Yes—when I called to collect the copy of *A Midwinter Night's Dream* from you.'

'But that was collected by a motorbike messenger.' Her eyes widened as she remembered the tall, black-clad figure. 'That was you?'

Ben grinned and nodded. 'It's much easier to get round London on a bike than by car.'

'Will you take me for a ride some time?'

It was Ben's turn to look surprised. 'Of course. Do you enjoy riding motorbikes?'

'I don't know; I've never been on one before. But I believe that you should try as many new things as you can, especially if you're a writer. Don't you?'

'Within limits,' Ben said in some amusement. 'Where shall I put this bottle?'

'The kitchen is in here. I'll take it, shall I?'

He followed her as she put the wine in the fridge and leaned against the door-jamb, watching as she took out a vase and started putting the flowers in it. He, too, had taken trouble with his appearance, was wearing well-cut casual clothes and looked lean and handsome. He said, 'There are some new experiences that you just shouldn't try if you know you're going to hate them, because always afterwards it will come through in your work.'

'You mean your own, personal preferences show through in your writing?'

'That's right. Don't you find that?' he asked.

Turning from her task, Nell leant back against the kitchen cabinets, her arms resting behind her as she thought about it. 'I can't say that I've consciously noticed it. I've always tried to keep apart from my work, look at it objectively and . . .' Her voice died away as she saw that Ben wasn't listening to her. His gaze was on her, his eyes dwelling on her thrusting chest, then moving slowly down her length and darkening with need. He licked lips gone dry and curled his hands into clenched fists.

Strangely flustered, Nell quickly straightened up and turned to finish the flowers. 'There! Don't they look good? Now, how about a drink? There's some cool sparkling wine or I have beer if you'd prefer it?'

'Wine would be great.'

Taking out the bottle, Nell let him open it, watching, noticing that he did it deftly and without fuss, laughing when he adroitly caught the cork as it exploded from the bottle. They went through into the sitting-room, sat down to chat, but Ben seemed restless and got up to look at the books she kept in waist-high shelving on the far wall.

'This is a nice place,' he said, looking round the room. 'But is this all you've got?'

'No, there's another floor upstairs. It's smaller than this, though, because the roof slopes away.'

He nodded, then took refuge in shop talk and said, 'How did you get on with the script today?'

'I didn't do much; I took the afternoon off. How did your meeting about the film go?'

'Fine. I've arranged for you to go to the television studios and watch a serial being made, by the way.'

'Great. When?'

'Some time next week.'

They chatted on until their drinks were finished, then Nell stood up and said, 'Are you hungry?'

His eyes were on her again and he said, 'Yes,' thickly, but it was for more than food.

They sat at the table, ate the meal, drank, talked, took their time. When it grew dusk outside Nell lit the candle and they talked across its soft, flickering glow. Their conversation was light, easy, and they hardly touched on personal subjects at all. But as the meal ended Nell could sense the growing tension in Ben, could see from the way he drew lines with his finger on the tablecloth that his ease of manner hid a scarcely controllable need.

When they'd finished their coffee, he leant forward and took hold of her hand. She stiffened, knowing what was to come, knowing what he expected. 'I want you, Nell,' he said flatly, but with a tremor in his tone.

'I rather gathered that,' she returned lightly.

'And so?' His chin came forward, eager, but taut against a possible rejection.

'We don't know much about each other,' she prevaricated.

Ben's mouth thinned. 'That means that you want to ask me some questions, I take it?'

She nodded.

'Are they so important? Couldn't we just ... ?' Then Ben gave her a wry look. 'Go on. Ask.'

'Did your wife leave you?'

His whole face immediately became an expressionless mask. 'I suppose you could say that. She died.'

Nell's breath caught in her throat in dismay. 'Oh! I——' She broke off, knowing he wouldn't want her pity or sympathy. 'When?' she said after a long moment.

'Over two years ago.'

'And have you ... ?'

'Have I had another woman since? No. I haven't.'

'My God! You must be as frustrated as hell!' she exclaimed involuntarily, and stared at him, her eyes large and appalled.

Ben looked at her, and to her surprise suddenly gave a huge grin. 'Yes, I'm afraid I am,' he admitted. 'Although I didn't know quite how much until I kissed you yesterday. Since then I've been able to think of little else.'

'Oh! Oh, I see.'

'And so?' he said again, his tone more forceful this time.

Nell bit her lip. 'I have to know on—on what sort of terms our—our relationship is going to be.'

'Relationship?'

'I don't know what else you'd call it.'

He kept hold of her hand but drew back a little, out of the candle's light, so that she couldn't see his face. 'I want you,' he said shortly. 'I like you and I'm very attracted to you. But I don't know you well enough to... It's too soon for me to make any kind of commitment.' He released her hand. 'If that's what you want then I'm sorry, but I can't——'

'It isn't what I want,' Nell broke in quickly. 'I wanted to hear you say that. I don't want a love-affair, just an uncomplicated, open relationship. No strings on either side.'

Ben leaned forward to look into her face. 'Just—just sex.'

'Yes.' She nodded. 'Just sex. And to be friends. That's all I'm willing to give.'

He frowned, looked almost as if he was going to argue, but then closed his eyes tightly for a moment before saying, 'Then that's what I'll take—and give in return.'

Reaching out, she put her hand back in his. 'So it's a bargain, then?'

That made him smile. 'Yes, a bargain.' But then the dark, hungry look came back into his eyes. Standing up, he picked up the candle. 'So why don't you show me where this bedroom of yours is?'

She led the way and drew the curtains, then Ben undressed her by the light of the candle. But as her clothes came off his hands began to tremble and his breath come in small groans of agonised anticipation. His breath was hot against her skin as he kissed her, the tension in his body impossible to control. Nell tried to help him, to unbutton his shirt, but he couldn't wait and tore it off, a button flying loose. His mouth was on hers, on her breasts, her throat, her skin. His hands clasped her waist, bruising her in their tremulous, greedy eagerness.

Throwing aside the last of their clothes, Ben propelled
her backwards on to the bed. His breath now was hoarse
and gasping, the driving force of his starved body impossible to deny. He came down on her, took her in a
savage frenzy of animal hunger, his head thrown back
in a great cry of excitement as his thrusting body reached
its overwhelming, burning climax of passion and desire.

It had been a selfish coupling, his body too long
starved of love for Ben to be able to consider Nell. He
slumped down beside her, his breath hoarse, the heart
hammering in his chest, his skin wet with sweat. Nell
lay still beside him, letting her own body recover, wondering what kind of lover he was. Was he always this
selfish, was she just to be used, or would he care about
her enough to make it good for her, too?

His lips found her bare shoulder, kissed it in tender
gratitude. 'Oh, Nell! Oh, Nell,' he murmured as soon
as he could speak.

It was a while longer, but not that long, before his
hands began gently to explore her, to caress the length
of her leg, the softness of her shoulders, the sensitive
curves of her breasts. 'You're so beautiful, Nell,' he
murmured. 'So small and perfect.'

She let him touch her wherever he wanted, just lay
back and let him find out what it was like to be in bed
with a woman again, enjoying his sighs of pleasure, his
smiles as he found that he had the power to make her
gasp with awareness. She was prepared for it to take a
time for him to want her again, but was willing to wait,
didn't in turn explore him because she knew it would
make him get excited that much more quickly. So she
was unprepared when he came on top of her and began
to kiss her body, his own hardening as his nostrils filled
with the perfume of her skin and his lips aroused an

answering desire in her. Ben gave a cry of pleasure as she began to pant, her body arching towards his, her hands gripping his shoulders. She moaned and her hips moved under his, yearning for fulfilment. He bent to kiss her mouth, using his hands and body to rouse her further, to make her cry out his name in longing.

Only then, when he knew she was on the brink of her own peak of excitement, did he take her again, and this time manage to defer his own pleasure to prolong hers, to lift her on a great roller-coaster of sensuality, a spiral of delight that reached its crescendo just as he was unable to hold out any longer and their voices joined in a cry of shared ecstasy.

The candle flickered for the last time and went out. Nell lay in the darkness, Ben's arm heavy across her, and felt a tear run down her cheek. It had been so good, better than she'd dared to hope. She had never known that her body could be lifted to such heights, her senses never so overwhelmed by sensuality. But then, she had never been in the hands of such an expert before, a man with enough experience to make her pleasure equal his own. His experience must have come from being married, she supposed, and wondered how long Ben and his wife had been together, and, fleetingly, how she'd died.

But Ben's past was of little importance now, not when she was lying in his arms, her body still trembling from the novelty of physical fulfilment. Nell felt supremely happy, and grateful for his skill, for his strength in over-coming his still great, urgent need so that she could reach her own peak of excitement. She wanted to tell him how good it had been, but knew that she didn't have to; he must surely have known from her reaction. Besides, if she started going on about how wonderful it had felt then he might become alarmed, be afraid that she might become possessive, or want to get too close. And she definitely didn't want to drive him away. That, above all, was certain.

He had fallen asleep; she could tell by Ben's regular breathing. It gave her time to decide how she was going to play it, how to conduct this new romance. They had both agreed that there were to be no strings; Ben obviously hadn't got over losing his wife yet and wasn't ready to make any commitments. And as for herself . . . Nell thought about it in the darkness. Years ago, when she'd left home at eighteen, she had made up her mind that all she wanted out of life was a successful career. No man had ever come along to make her have second thoughts; most of them were so selfish, both in bed and out of it, that they'd only strengthened her resolve. And there was certainly no way she wanted to take on a ready-made family, some other woman's child. To do so would be a cruel irony after she'd had to give up her own baby.

But she had to admit that she was greatly attracted to Ben. She wouldn't be here with him otherwise. And it wasn't all physical. She liked and respected him on an intellectual level. He was a good writer, and an unselfish teacher; she'd learnt a lot from him these last weeks. And it looked as if she was going to learn a lot from him that she hadn't expected, Nell thought with a chuckle. But it wasn't all one-sided; she knew that she'd given him great pleasure, too. Knew that he would always remember tonight, because it had been so long since he'd been with a woman. Idly she wondered why, if he was that frustrated, Ben hadn't found someone else before now. He was still young, good-looking, successful; it wouldn't have been hard for him to meet someone. So why her?

Nell couldn't think why, and didn't much care. She was just grateful that he had, that it had been so good. So now all she had to worry about was keeping him around for a while. And to do that, she decided, she must keep things light, not get emotional or possessive in any way, perhaps even be offhand. And one thing was for sure: she had to make it as good for him as it had been for her.

These decisions made, Nell put them into operation at once. She blew into his ear, then began to tickle him. Ben twitched and moved, but his eyes stayed closed. Her hand moved on to tickle him in places people didn't usually get tickled. That made him gasp and he chuckled softly.

'Are you going to sleep all night?' she said in a grumbly voice.

'Minx.' Then he gasped again. 'Hey!'

'You want me to stop?'

'God, no!'

That made her laugh and she propped herself on one elbow so that she could lean over and kiss him. 'I suppose you know you're much too tall?'

'I'll cut my legs off,' he offered.

'As long as it's only your legs.'

Ben gave a burst of laughter, then put his arms round her, pulling her close. On a suddenly fierce note he said, 'Teach me how to laugh again, Nell. My sweet Nell.'

Putting her hands on either side of his face, she kissed him gently but deeply, then said, 'OK, Buster, you asked for it,' and began to tickle him until he laughed and protested his way into submission and then lay back and let her make love to him.

They slept then, both satiated by love, Nell held in the curve of his arms. But in the early hours of the morning she woke and moved into a more comfortable position. Ben stirred and reached for her in his sleep. 'Lucy,' he murmured. 'Lucy, my love.'

Nell was up first the next morning, had showered and dressed before Ben woke up. When he came down to join her, his hair still damp from the shower, he looked like someone who'd just been set free from a prison. The tiredness was gone from his face, and there was a glow of elated triumph in his grey eyes. Coming up behind her, he enfolded her in a bear hug and kissed her neck. 'Good morning, beautiful.' Turning her round, he smiled into her eyes. 'Thank you for last night. Thank you, thank you, thank you.' And he kissed her each time he said it.

Teasing him, Nell said, 'Last night? Did something happen last night?'

'Well, if it didn't I've been having the most amazing dreams.' Sitting down on a chair, he pulled her on to his lap. 'But next time don't get up so early in the morning.'

'Next time?' She raised her eyebrows. 'So there's going to be a next time, is there?'

'You bet your life on it,' Ben said, so forcefully that he made her laugh.

'Anyone would think you enjoyed it,' she remarked, wanting to provoke him into saying so.

His lips found her mouth, took hers in little, demanding kisses. 'Well, if you weren't sure, I'd be happy to demonstrate again,' he offered.

Nell laughed but pushed herself up on her feet. 'I'm a working girl, remember. And my boss is a hard taskmaster. What would you like for breakfast?'

'Everything you've got. I can't ever remember feeling so hungry.'

Nell smiled, but it made her wonder about his wedding night, although he and his wife—his Lucy, who still haunted his dreams—might not have waited until then. Did any engaged couple nowadays? Nell found that she had a great curiosity about his wife, about the life they'd shared in the flat. But that wouldn't do; he'd been reluctant enough to answer the few questions she'd asked last night. And she'd learnt little enough; just the bare bones of his tragedy. She must put his wife out of her mind and concentrate only on the present.

She cooked a full English breakfast for him, but contented herself with just scrambled eggs on toast. Sitting down opposite, she said, 'You spent the night here.'

Ben's left eyebrow rose in amusement. 'I know.'

'So what about Mark?'

'I hired a woman from an agency to sit with him. Someone we'd had before, so Mark knew her.'

'She might have got worried when you didn't come home,' Nell pointed out.

A mischievous, almost boyish look came into Ben's eyes. 'Er—no. I told her I might not be able to get back.'

'That sure of me, were you?' Nell said, contriving a look of hurt embarrassment.

'No.' Ben reached out and covered her hand. 'But I was darn sure what *I* wanted.'

She smiled into his eyes. 'And pretty sure that I wanted it, too.'

Ben sighed. 'It's a great pity we have to work today.'

'But we have a script to finish,' she pointed out. After finishing her breakfast, Nell ran upstairs to make the bed and tidy up. She had already cleared the dishes and everything from last night, and the flat was as neat as always.

'A woman's touch,' Ben said when she put the breakfast things away.

He had spoken lightly enough but when Nell glanced at him she saw that a shadow had saddened his face. 'What I need is a man's touch,' she remarked, adding, when she saw him start to grin, 'To put up shelves and fix leaking taps and things. I have to pay the earth to carpenters and plumbers. Are you any good at that kind of thing?'

'So long as it isn't a major construction job, I can cope.'

'Good. I'll make you a list.'

She smiled up at him and Ben took her in his arms and kissed her. But how different his embrace was now. The desperate quality had gone and in its place was sensuous enjoyment, knowledge, and the beginnings of possessiveness. It was far more leisurely and without any passionate hunger, but it evoked the night that had gone and the fulfilment they'd found in each other's arms.

'You're really something, you know that?' Ben murmured.

Nell knew exactly what he meant but said, 'For a writer, that's a very ambiguous remark.'

'Writers don't always make good speakers.'

'Work on it,' she instructed him, which made him chuckle.

His eyes full of amusement, he said, 'I think this is going to be fun.'

'Of course it is.' She broke away from him. 'Let's go.'

They drove back to Ben's flat in his car. As she'd noticed before, it was an estate car, but now she saw that quite a few of Mark's things were in it: a skateboard, a small cycle, and a cricket set, which explained why Ben drove a family car. The child-minder, a cheerful middle-aged woman, had given Mark his breakfast and was sitting watching television with him, something she seemed to be enjoying more than Mark was. He ran to meet them as they arrived and Ben swept him up into his arms.

'Hello, old son.'

Mark put his arms round Ben's neck and clung to him tightly. 'You didn't come home,' he said reproachfully.

'I told you I might not be able to. You know I have to go away sometimes. You were all right with Mrs Goodwin, weren't you?'

But Mark refused to be placated and clung to Ben as he carried him into the sitting-room. Mrs Goodwin greeted Ben and gave Nell a look brimful of curiosity.

'This is my colleague, Miss Marsden,' Ben introduced. 'I collected her on the way here.'

'I brought you some biscuits, Mark,' Nell said. 'Have you got a tin we can put them in?'

Mark consented to be put down and went with Nell to the kitchen while Ben paid Mrs Goodwin. When she'd gone Ben came down to the kitchen to join them so Nell tactfully left father and son together for a while.

It was another lovely day. Nell found a lounger and took it out into the garden, envying Ben his few square yards of greenness. She found the daily paper and caught up on the latest news and gossip until Ben came out to find her.

'Is Mark OK?' she asked.

'Yes, fine. He feels insecure if I go away now.'

He didn't say since his wife had died, Nell noticed. 'You mean that he's afraid of losing you, too?'

Ben glanced at her, a slightly cautious look in his eyes. 'Something like that.'

He was obviously reluctant to discuss it, but Nell wanted them to be open with each other, so she said, 'It's natural enough, I suppose. It must be very hard for a child to lose a parent. Especially a child so young. And it must be difficult for you not to over-compensate.'

'It's held him back,' Ben said shortly. 'He's immature for his age.'

'You said he was nearly seven, didn't you?'

'Yes, he'll be seven in September.'

September. Nell's face paled a little. So Mark had been born in the same month and year as her own son. 'What date in September?' she managed to ask.

'The tenth.'

Nell had never known the exact date of her baby's birth, but it was within a day or two of the tenth. Her hands tightened on the newspaper, and she changed the subject abruptly, pointing out a show-business item to Ben. They discussed it for a while, Ben accepting the change without question, perhaps with relief, then they went inside to start work.

During the course of the morning he rang a friend at the film studios he'd told her about and arranged for them to go and watch the serial being made on Monday.

'What are you doing for the weekend?' he asked her.

'I have a date tomorrow night, but apart from that nothing definite. My options are open.'

'Should I be jealous of your date?' Ben asked, his eyebrow rising.

'Are you the kind of man that gets jealous?' she parried.

Reaching out, he took hold of her hand. 'Jealous enough not to want to share you with anyone else,' Ben said firmly.

'You're not. I'm not that kind of girl.'

'I'm glad to hear it.'

'Did you think I was?' she asked curiously.

'No.' Ben shook his head in a definite negative. 'The opposite. You have a kind of "keep your distance" air about you. That first time I kissed you I quite expected to get my face slapped.'

'You might have done—if you hadn't taken me completely by surprise, and if...'

'And if?' Ben prompted when she paused.

Her eyes came up to meet his. 'And if I hadn't been wondering what it would be like to be kissed by you.'

'So you weren't immune to me,' Ben said, a pleased grin on his face.

'Did you think I was?'

'You didn't exactly give me a great deal of encouragement.'

'I invited you to dinner,' she reminded him.

'To a dinner *party* with a load of other people. And so casually. Take it or leave it. And on the very weekend when I'd arranged to take Mark to my mother's!' He shook his head ruefully. 'I thought you were just being kind, taking pity on a lonely man who couldn't cook.'

'I was,' Nell admitted. 'Then.'

'And now?' His voice sharpened a little. 'Are you still being kind, Nell?'

'Of course.' Her answer brought his head up and his jaw tightened. But then she said smilingly, 'To myself.'

That made him grin and he said, 'I had an idea you quite enjoyed it last night.'

'You could be right at that.'

Leaning forward, he kissed her lingeringly, savouring her mouth, the pliant softness of her lips. 'Nell, my sweet Nell,' he breathed. 'I want to make love to you again.'

'You do?' she murmured, eyes closed, her head lifting so that he could kiss the long column of her throat.

Ben reached across and pulled her on to his lap, the console in front of them forgotten. His voice thickening, he said, 'I want to take you out into the garden, to lay you on the grass and take your clothes off. To look at you and then make love to you with the sun hot on our bodies.'

His hand went inside her shirt, found her nipple and began to tease it. Nell moaned and moved on his lap, exciting him even more. Her nails dug into his shoulders as need grew deep within her, and she said shudderingly, 'Do it, then. Do it.'

His kiss deepened into searing, heated passion and Ben put his arms round her as if to lift her up and carry her outside. But then he became still and after a moment put his hand behind her head and held her against his shoulder. She could feel the wild beating of his heart as it slowly stilled, almost taste his chagrin. 'Not here,' he said. 'Mark is here.'

Nell slid from his lap on to her own chair. 'You even daydream fiction,' she remarked wryly.

'I'm sorry. I got carried away.'

'And took me with you,' she said softly, looking into his eyes.

He still had hold of her hand and at that his grip tightened convulsively. '*Nell*!' he said forcefully. Just that, just her name. But with such emphasis that it expressed his overwhelming need, his disappointment, his frustration and regret.

There was a noise outside in the corridor and she quickly swung round towards the desk, aware of her flushed cheeks. Mark came in, carrying a toy, 'Dad, my rocket ship won't work.'

Ben took it from him, concentrated on it. 'It looks as if the battery has run out. Can you find a spare one in the cupboard, do you think?' He took out the old battery and gave it to the boy. 'One like this, with these numbers on.'

Mark went off obediently. They looked at each other, both aware that if the child had come in five minutes earlier he would have caught them kissing. 'It's difficult,' Ben said ruefully.

Nell felt like saying that Mark would eventually have to accept that his father had formed a new relationship, but she held her tongue; it was up to Ben to make his own decision about telling the boy. And it was early days yet, the very first day in fact. So she merely said, 'We'd better get back to work, then. Where were we?'

But instead of looking at the monitor Ben said, 'You were going to tell me who that date was with.'

That pleased her and made her laugh. 'It's a party to celebrate the end of taping a radio serial I worked on.'

'And are you taking an escort along?'

She shook her head. 'It isn't that kind of party.'

'Good.' He put a hand on her bare arm, stroked it gently with his finger, wanting to touch her. 'If I can get someone to look after Mark this weekend, can you spend it with me?'

'Yes, of course.'

The certainty of her reply, and all that it promised, did wonders for his ego. Ben gave a happy, mock-lascivious grin, put his arms round her in a fierce hug and growled like a bear, making her laugh delightedly.

'Dad?' Neither of them had heard Mark come back. He caught hold of Ben's sleeve and pulled his arm down, then glowered at Nell.

'Have you found the battery? Here, let me put it in for you.' Ben kept his voice matter-of-fact as he picked up the toy. 'Nell and I were trying out the story we're writing.'

'Yes, I was supposed to be attacked by a grizzly bear,' Nell backed him up.

'But you were laughing,' Mark said accusingly.

'I know; I'm a rotten actress.'

He gave her a suspicious look, not knowing whether to believe them or not, and from then on played on the patio just outside the window, where he could keep an eye on them.

They all went out to lunch, to a hamburger bar of Mark's choice, and he carefully sat between them. Ben gave her a rueful look over the boy's head and she shrugged in return. Nell guessed that neither of them really knew how to behave in the situation. It was new to both of them to have a small boy acting as gooseberry. Ben was hungry for her again, and wanted to touch her and kiss her, and Nell, too, wanted that. It was natural after their closeness of last night. To not even be able to hold hands was frustrating to say the least. And she really didn't see why they couldn't; it had been two years since Ben's wife had died so surely Mark must have got over it by now. Surely he couldn't resent his father's friendship with another woman?

But it seemed that he did; this child of six acted like some old-fashioned chaperon, not leaving them alone together again all the afternoon, and made such a fuss when Ben suggested leaving him with some friends for the weekend that the idea had to be abandoned. 'Mark went into a tantrum,' Ben said ruefully when he phoned Nell on the Friday evening, just before she left for her party. 'Threw himself on the floor and kicked and screamed. Then, when I got angry, he burst into tears and clung to me, begging me not to leave him. I had to promise I wouldn't, Nell. There was nothing else I could do. I'm sorry.'

'It's OK. I understand.' Nell tried to hide her disappointment, to sound genuinely sympathetic.

'There are reasons for Mark being so possessive.' She thought he was going to tell her but Ben paused, then said with a sigh, 'I'm going to miss being with you, Nell.'

There was an obvious answer to that; he could ask her to go and stay with him at his flat, or at least for them all to go out together so that Mark could get used to her being around. Nell waited for him to say it, but he didn't. Hurt, she said almost offhandedly, 'I'll see you on Monday, then, when we go to the television studios at Borehamwood.'

'Yes. I've decided to take Mark down to the friends I was going to leave him with and stay there with him. They have children of their own, so I'm hoping he'll enjoy himself and be willing to stay by himself some other time. God, I hope he does,' he said, so fervently that she was placated. 'I can't wait to make love to you again, Nell.'

She chuckled softly. 'Making up for lost time, huh?'

'Definitely!'

They talked until Nell had to leave. The radio series had been successful so everyone at the party was happy and relaxed. Nell enjoyed it, both socially and for some new contacts she made. She caught up with the show-biz gossip, and was much envied when people found out she was working on a serial—and especially when they heard she was collaborating with Benet Rigby. Nell hugged to herself the compliments paid to him, accepting them almost as something personal now that they were lovers. Or at least had spent one night together; heaven knew when they would be able to again now that Mark was acting up. Perhaps Ben ought to be firmer with the child, she thought, but then shrugged mentally; she mustn't be selfish; Ben's first consideration must always be for his son. She knew that and accepted it, so would just have to be patient and let Ben sort it out. But that night together had added a whole new dimension to her life and she longed to be in his arms again.

Her wish was granted much sooner than she expected. Ben hadn't called during the weekend and on Sunday Nell went to bed with a book, trying to take her mind off her frustration, but at ten-thirty her doorbell rang.

Slipping on a robe over her thin nightdress, Nell went barefooted down the stairs and switched on the light in the hall. The door was solid and she had to open it on the chain before she could see who was there. Outside stood a tall, dark-clad figure, a visored helmet on his head, a motorbike standing at the kerb. This time Nell had no difficulty in recognising him. She gave a whoop of delighted surprise, took off the chain and pulled the door wide. Ben strode in, kicked the door shut behind him, then pulled off the helmet and tossed it aside before grabbing her and kissing her, his whole body already tense with anticipation. Still kissing her, he picked her up in his arms and carried her up the stairs and into her bedroom.

Black leather gear was thrown all over the floor as they both struggled to get it off him as fast as possible—not easy when they were at the same time kissing each other in ever-increasing passion and excitement. In the end, unable to wait another second, Ben simply grabbed her and pulled her down on to the bed, to make love to her in frenzied, surging hunger that lifted them both to the heights of passion.

Afterwards, when she'd got her breath back, Nell laughed delightedly. 'How on earth did you manage to get here?'

'I sneaked away after Mark had gone to bed. I made him play very energetic games all day so that he would be tired out.'

'You haven't left him at home by himself?'

Ben pressed her shoulder reassuringly. 'No, he's still with my friends. I—er—sort of explained the situation and they agreed to hang on to him until tomorrow evening for me.'

'You told them you had a pressing engagement, did you?'

He chuckled richly. 'And how! I've been able to think of nothing but this all weekend.'

'Of this?'

He recognised the note in her voice and put up a hand to stroke her hair. 'Of you. Making love, yes, but wanting to be with you.'

She nodded, content again. 'I've been so frustrated, too. I now know what that saying means—you can't have too much of a good thing.'

Ben burst into laughter. 'Well, thank you for the compliment, ma'am!'

'You're very welcome, sir. Do you realise we still have some clothes on—and those studs are lethal?'

They soon put that right and lay close until they made love again. That night Ben didn't call out for his wife in his sleep.

In the morning it was he who woke Nell, kissing her into awareness, pulling back the covers and caressing her length, his skin like silk against hers. Now his love-making was slow, almost languorous, and was all for her pleasure. Nell had never known that ecstasy could be so prolonged, that her body could be brought so close to so many peaks of excitement and then away again, only to return at a higher level of delight. She hadn't known that her body had so many places that were sensitive to a delicate touch, to the warmth of a kiss, that it could respond like an instrument to this most skilful of players. It was exquisite, sensational, and afterwards Nell rolled on to her stomach and stretched out like a contented cat, her mind still in a dreamlike state of absolute bliss.

After a while Ben said, 'Would you like a coffee?'

She shook her head, her eyes still closed, and heard him pad to the kitchen. It was daylight now, the sun shining through the curtains. Nell knew that some time soon she would have to come down to reality, but not yet, not quite yet.

Ben came back and she could smell the coffee that he always took strong and black. He kissed her shoulder and sat on the bed while he drank it. 'I hope Mark's all right,' he murmured.

'You were going to tell me about him,' Nell said, without opening her eyes.

'What about him?'

'Why he's so possessive.'

'Possessive? Was that the word I used?'

'Yes, I think so.'

He was silent for a moment, then she heard him sigh and put the cup down on the bedside cabinet. 'It isn't his fault if he is. He's actually much better than he was at first. You see, he's afraid.' Ben paused for a long moment, and she understood why when he said shortly, 'My wife was killed in a car accident. Mark was with her. She was driving and he was in his special seat in the back. In a way it was his fault that the accident happened; he'd been playing up and trying to undo the straps. She told him off and he threw one of his toys at her just as she glanced back to see if he was all right. It hit her in the eye, blinded her.' His voice grew harsh. 'She hit a lorry.'

Nell was fully awake now, appalled by what he was saying. 'How do you know this?' she asked when he didn't go on.

'She was near to her parents' house. Her mother got to the hospital before she died, heard her say what had happened.' Bitterly, he added, 'Then the stupid woman turned on Mark and told him he'd killed his mother.'

'Oh, no!'

'Or rather she told him that he'd killed her daughter—she also told him, all at the same time, that Lucy wasn't his real mother.'

'Not his mother?'

'No. In one sentence she completely ruined Mark's life; she told him that not only had he killed Lucy, but also that he was only an adopted child and that his real mother hadn't wanted him!'

CHAPTER FIVE

NELL was so stunned by what Ben had told her that for a couple of minutes she could only stare at him. The word 'adopted' filled her brain. A boy born in the same year, the same month, as her own child—and now she found out that he, too, had been adopted. It was too much of a coincidence! Mark could be hers, her son!

'I'm not surprised you're speechless,' Ben was saying. 'I couldn't believe it either, when I found out. It was all such a mess,' he said bitterly, remembering. 'I had to deal with Lucy being killed, my mother-in-law in a dreadful state... And there was Mark huddled on the floor in a corner, refusing to let anyone touch him, not crying, just—sort of frozen. It was several weeks before he would even speak. I took him to a child psychiatrist and she found out what had happened. I could have killed Lucy's mother for that,' he ground out forcefully.

'It was very cruel, admittedly,' Nell said slowly, trying to cut through the numbness in her brain. 'But she'd just lost her own child, hadn't she?'

Ben nodded morosely. 'Yes. Lucy was her only daughter. But she had no right to say that to Mark. No right at all. God, he was only four!'

The anger in his voice made her realise that she mustn't think about her own worries now; somehow she had to put it all out of her mind and concentrate on Ben. Sitting up, Nell managed to pull herself together enough to put her arms round him and kiss his head. 'My poor Ben, what a time you've had.'

He tensed and turned quickly to look at her. 'I didn't tell you all that because I wanted your pity.'

She smiled a little. 'That's good, because all I was offering was sympathy. You and Mark have had rotten luck. But as you said, Mark is much better than he was—and you seem to have recovered quite a bit, too.'

For a moment or two he wasn't sure how to take that, but as he was naked in bed beside her he could hardly help but admit that it was true. 'I feel a different person since I met you, Nell,' he told her, and planted a kiss on her nose.

'Am I really the first girl you've been attracted to since you lost your wife?' she asked, wanting to distract them both from traumatic subjects.

'Yes.' He lay back on the pillow and looked up at her. 'For the first fifteen months or so I just shut myself away in the flat with Mark and worked. I hardly met any women—except those of mine and Lucy's so-called friends who decided to come round and offer me ''comfort'' as they called it.'

'Really?' Nell looked at him with interest. 'Even right at the beginning?'

'Oh, yes. A couple within the first month.'

'You could base a plot round that,' Nell murmured, a distant look in her eyes.

Ben pulled her down beside him and gave her a mock-punch on the jaw. 'Forever a writer, aren't you? I'm supposed to be answering your question, woman!'

'Sorry. Go on.'

It seemed that now Ben had started to confide in her he wanted to tell her everything, because he went on, 'During that first year I went out of my way to avoid women, especially married ones with young children. I resented their happiness; why should they be alive when

Lucy was dead? That kind of thing. I'm afraid I turned many of our friends, even the genuine ones who only wanted to help, against me.'

'Didn't they understand?'

'Oh, yes, I'm back on good terms with most of them now.' He smiled wryly. 'Recently I've been receiving lots of dinner invitations and finding myself paired off with some girl my hostess hopes to match me up with.'

'But you haven't succumbed?'

'No. My libido hadn't been even remotely stirred until I called round here to collect that book and you opened the door to me.'

'Really?' She rested an elbow on his chest and looked into his eyes. She wasn't altogether sure that she believed him; after two years Ben must have been ripe for an affair. Maybe they had been thrown together at just the right time.

'Really,' he assured her. 'And when we began to work together I found that you interested me more and more.'

'You were intrigued by my brains and personality, of course,' she teased.

'Oh, definitely.' He put out a hand to cup her breast, toyed with the rosy nipple. 'The fact that you have a gorgeous little body and such beautiful brown eyes didn't come into it one little bit.'

Nell wrinkled her nose at him. 'That's what I like about you,' she mocked. 'Not a chauvinistic bone in your body.'

Ben grabbed her at that and pulled her underneath him, would have made love to her again except that she rolled quickly out of bed and headed for the bathroom.

'Hey, where are you going?'

'We have to go to the television studios this morning. Have you forgotten?'

'We have time. Come back.'

She looked at him round the bathroom door and gave a cheeky grin. 'Haven't you heard that expression entertainers use—always leave them wanting more?'

Turning on the shower, Nell stood under it and at last was able to give free rein to her thoughts and fears. Was Mark her child, *was* he? But no, it was impossible. There must have been lots of boys born in that month who'd been given for adoption. And besides, she had lived miles away from London; her son was hardly likely to have been given to a couple who lived so far away. Unless adoption agencies made a point of doing that, so that there was no danger of mother and child running into each other. She remembered that she'd thought Mark rather short for his age, especially when Ben was so tall. Well, that was explained now, but she realised miserably that she was quite short so her own son might well be so.

Lifting up her hands, Nell put them on either side of her head, trying to shut out the thoughts. This is crazy, she told herself. It would be a chance in a million. In a billion. But surely there couldn't have been that many little boys adopted that month. The thought wouldn't go away, no matter how hard she tried to shut it out.

Then she tried to be logical, asking herself why did it matter anyway. OK, so there was a possibility that Mark could be hers. So what? What difference did it make? She had given her child away and that was the end of it. She had no right to—— Yes, I do damn well have a right! her mind screamed. I have a right to think about him and wonder, to worry that he's well and happy. And Mark certainly isn't happy; he's hurting inside. And maybe I could help him...

'Nell! Are you about finished in there?' Ben banged on the door.

'Two minutes,' she called back, and hastily soaped herself.

She came back into the bedroom with a bath-sheet wrapped round her, a towel over her wet hair. For a moment a look of pain came into Ben's eyes, and she intuitively knew that for an instant he had been reminded of his wife. Well, that was bound to happen, she supposed. Until he got used to being around a woman again, got used to her. Making an almost visible effort, he smiled and said, 'Do you always take that long in the shower?'

'Long?' She raised her eyebrows. 'You think that was long? You should be around when I have a bath.'

'I would very much like to be around when you have a bath.' He grinned and put his hands on her arms. 'You smell delicious. Clean and fresh and young.' He kissed her shoulder, little kisses that danced along her skin. 'How big is your bath?' he said suggestively.

Laughing, Nell pushed him away. 'Go take a look. Are you hungry? I know I am. I'll make breakfast while you shower.'

She found her robe and put it on while she efficiently cooked breakfast. When Ben joined her she said, 'I expect you want to phone to see if Mark's OK, don't you?'

Ben glanced at his watch. 'It's a bit early; I'll leave it for another half-hour.' He had put on a towel, sarong-style, and they sat in informal intimacy as they ate, then went back upstairs to the bedroom to dress.

Nell was aware that Ben watched her as she did so, his eyes on her legs as she smoothed stockings over them and did up the suspenders.

'I'm glad you wear stockings instead of tights,' he commented. 'Much more sexy.'

She smiled but didn't speak, instead standing in just her underwear, grey and lacy, in front of the dressing-table mirror to blow-dry her hair. Although he wasn't directly behind her she could see Ben's reflection; he was standing by the bed while he dressed, sorting out the clothes that had been thrown off last night. But he kept looking towards her and the bleak look was back in his eyes. This must be one of the reasons why he'd avoided women, she guessed. To see a woman dressing, doing everyday, personal things, must be very poignant for him, would tear at his heart until he got used to it.

To make it easier for him, she finished dressing and making-up quickly, chatting to him the while about their proposed trip to the studios, then let him go downstairs alone to make his phone call while she tidied the bedroom and bathroom.

'How was he?' she asked brightly, when she came down.

Ben gave a small shrug. 'Not very happy when he found I was gone. But I spoke to him and promised I'd pick him up tonight.'

Nell nodded, her feelings now terribly mixed. Yesterday she'd thought that Ben ought to be firmer with Mark, but now that she'd found out what a terrible time the child had been through, and even more because there was a remote chance he might be her son, she felt that Ben ought not to let him out of his sight.

'I'll have to go back to my place to change,' Ben remarked. 'Would you like to follow in a taxi or will you risk a ride on the bike?'

'Oh, the bike of course—but I don't have a helmet.'

'That's OK, I have a spare.'

He went to get it and they set off through the traffic-clogged streets, Nell clinging to his back as Ben weaved between the lanes of cars, heading north and soon reaching more open roads as they went in the opposite direction to all the commuters heading into central London.

'How was that?' he asked when they arrived at his building.

Nell took off the helmet and shook out her hair. 'Absolutely great! But it must be even better when you get on a motorway and can go really fast?'

'Speed merchant,' he grinned. He held out a bunch of keys to her. 'Why don't you go on in while I put the bike away round the back?'

The flat seemed strangely empty when she let herself in. Going into the cloakroom, Nell combed her hair and checked her make-up. Ben came in and went, whistling, to his bedroom. While she waited for him Nell wandered into the front sitting-room, the room that was seldom used. Before she'd only peeped in the door but now she went right in and this time saw the photos grouped on a table near the window. The largest was a wedding photo of Ben and his wife. Nell picked it up to look more closely and saw that Lucy had been tall and blonde, with looks that Nell thought of as classy: rather thin-faced and aristocratic, but with a warm, outgoing smile. Looking at it, Nell could see immediately why Ben had been attracted—no, had allowed himself to be attracted—to her, to Nell herself: because she was the complete opposite to his wife. With someone small and dark there was far less danger of turning in an unwary moment and being reminded of his willowy blonde wife. Had it been a deliberate choice or a subconscious one? Nell wondered. But even so, this morning there had been moments when intimacy had brought its own memories, impossible to foresee, impossible to avoid. Carefully replacing the photograph in its exact position, Nell went out into the hall to wait for Ben.

They drove further north, heading along the dual carriageway through the suburbs and into more open country, found the television studios in what must once have been a sprawling village but was now almost a small town of shops and housing estates. Ben had arranged for them to watch a detective series being filmed, and they arrived just as shooting was about to start, the actors having already been made-up and the sets built and dressed. They sat at the back, out of the way, and Ben borrowed a script so that Nell could see for herself how the directions were put into use.

Normally Nell would have been immediately absorbed but today she had other things on her mind and found it difficult to concentrate at first; only after they'd been there for an hour or so did instructions like 'Cut away', 'Cheat', and 'Two shot' begin to have a real meaning.

They stayed at the studios the whole morning and Ben introduced her to several of the production crew that he knew, describing her as his co-writer, which pleased her a lot. Nell would have liked to stay for lunch at the studios but Ben gave a look of horror when she suggested it and said very firmly that they were going to a pub. They found one not too far away and ordered salads which they took out into the garden. It was quite late for lunch and most of the customers had gone back to work so they had the place more or less to themselves. It was another good day, more hazy than the past week, as if the weather was about to break, but still very warm.

At first they chatted about the serial they'd watched being made, but Nell's mind drifted and presently Ben said, 'Penny for them?'

She looked up, gave a smile of apology. 'Sorry.'

'Have you had an idea?'

'An idea?'

'When I get an idea for a plot or a story I tend to forget about everything else,' Ben explained. 'I have to concentrate on it and try to develop the idea while it's in my mind.'

'In case you lose it; I know the feeling. I'm sure I've lost some really good ideas because I've been distracted before I could write them down,' Nell agreed.

'I hope I haven't just done that.'

'No.' She shook her head.

'So what were you thinking about?'

It was difficult to answer. She'd been thinking of Mark, of course, but she could hardly tell him why. She hadn't yet given much thought to that, to what Ben's reaction might be if he ever found out her fears. Now her anxiety was all for Mark, but whether it was wise to say anything she wasn't at all sure.

She hesitated for too long; Ben gave her a sharp look and said, 'Is anything the matter, Nell?'

'Not really. It's just that...' She gave him a frowning glance. 'What you told me about Mark; he must need you very badly.'

'Yes, he does.'

'But last night—you left him to come to me.'

'Oh, I see. Are you saying that I ought not to have done?' She didn't answer and he gave a short, mirthless laugh and leaned forward to take her hand. 'I've done everything I can for Mark, devoted the last two years to him. But I can't let him govern my life. It isn't good for him and it certainly isn't good for me. He's at school now and is getting along well. He has the company of his contemporaries. Since meeting you I've realised just how badly I needed some company in my life—some adult female company,' he added with a smile, and raised her hand to kiss it lightly.

But Nell refused to be side-tracked. 'You said he was upset this morning,' she pointed out.

'Yes, but I reassured him. I want him to get used to the idea of my not being around all the time. There are bound to be times when I have to go away for a while, you know. It's in the nature of the job.'

'Yes, I suppose so. But...' she hesitated and gave him an uncertain look ' ...I don't want to be made to feel guilty about Mark every time you spend time with me.'

The hand holding hers suddenly tensed, his grip hurting. 'Are you saying that you want to end it?' Ben demanded, his jaw taut.

'I'm saying that you must put Mark first. Before yourself, and definitely before me.'

'Do you want to end it?' he insisted, his face grim.

Nell looked into his eyes and said, 'No! Of course I don't. But I don't want to feel that——'

'Don't worry about Mark,' Ben broke in. 'It's sweet of you and I appreciate your concern, but I do know what I'm doing. Believe me. Do you really think that I would hurt Mark after all he's been through? But for both our sakes I have to push him out of the nest a little, let him see that I have a life and friends of my own, too.'

Feeling the pressure of his hand, realising that Ben's new-found confidence was still shaky, Nell knew that she had to back down. 'Yes, of course. I'm sorry. It's—it's really nothing to do with me.'

'No, don't say that. I'm not telling you off, Nell. Of course it will concern you if—well, if things stay the way they are between us. I'm not trying to shut you out, but I do know what's best for Mark.'

'Of course,' Nell agreed. 'Oh, look! A squirrel. Do you think it might eat some bread?'

And so she was able to change the conversation, but, looking back on it afterwards, she thought that Ben *was* trying to shut her out. And she could understand why. Having an affair with her had done wonders for his morale, his confidence where women were concerned, but he still had a long way to go before he would be completely at ease with a woman, with any type of woman, again. He needed her now, because she was so different from his wife and could give him the stimulation he needed to push him back into a normal life. And he needed to feel wanted, too, as a lover, as a man. At the moment he was vulnerable; he'd proved that by being so afraid that she wanted to end it.

But Nell thought that eventually he would end it himself. She wasn't his type, if his wife was anything to go by. One day he would feel confident enough to go out and find himself another tall blonde girl. And where would that leave her? Especially in relation to Mark.

I have to find out who Mark is, she thought fiercely. *I have to know*.

They went back to the television studios for another hour or so after lunch, and Ben took her round to see the stages, the make-up rooms, where the props and costumes were kept, everything. It was fascinating, especially when they looked at costumes for the period in which their own serial was to be set.

'Will they make new costumes?' Nell asked. 'Or will we have to use some of these?'

'They might make new ones for the main characters, but they'll probably adapt some of these for the minor roles. Saves quite a bit of money that way.'

They left shortly afterwards, having thanked Ben's friend who'd arranged the visit, and got in the car again.

'It's too nice to go back to London,' Ben said. 'How would you like to drive through the countryside for a while?'

Nell nearly said what about Mark, but managed to stop herself. She must react just as any girlfriend would. So she turned to him with a smile and said, 'Great.'

They didn't go that far. Ben pulled into the gateway of a field off a narrow lane. They left the car and climbed the gate, Ben putting his hands on her waist to help Nell down. He kissed her, of course, his lips eager, then took her hand and led her across the meadow on the other side to the shade of a tree. The meadow was thick with wild flowers: the yellow of buttercups and mauve of clover. They smelt rich and heady when Ben laid her down in the long grass.

She hadn't thought he would want to go this far. With Mark on her mind she said, 'Ben, ought we to...?'

But he silenced her with kisses hot with need and she yielded to them, unable to resist. Ben put some flowers in her hair, and when he'd taken off her clothes he picked some more and let them trickle through his fingers on to her bare body.

Picking up a buttercup, he trailed it along her length, the gold of the petals reflecting on her skin. 'You're beautiful, Nell,' he said thickly. 'Exquisite.' Bending, he kissed her breasts, the scent of the flowers strong in his nostrils, the petals brushing his cheeks.

Nell put her hands on his shoulders and looked up at the sky, watched a bird wheeling above them, until her

mouth opened on a long moan of rapture. His mouth
moved on down her body, soft, exploring. Nell could
feel the heat on her skin, felt her pulses begin to race,
knew a deep, unbearable ache of longing, of physical
need. He moved up to caress her breasts again, feeling
the nipples harden under his lips, and circling them with
his tongue. So erotic, so sensuous. He had been gentle
with her, almost languid, but then, unable to take it any
more, she bit his shoulder, making Ben give a stifled cry
and suddenly become fiercely passionate. They rolled
on the grass, crushing the flowers, each trying to outdo
the other in giving pleasure. Legs entwined, his hands
on either side of her head, Ben kissed her compulsively.
But then he was over her and crying out her name,
thrusting forward, the sheen of perspiration on his skin,
his breath rasping in his throat as Nell arched towards
him, giving him her body with the eagerness he craved.

A bee buzzed near her head. Nell lifted a languid hand
and brushed it away. Ben was lying half on her, half on
the grass, his breathing slowly getting back to normal,
the beat of his heart gradually quietening. It had been
so good. Wonderful. But then, every time they made
love seemed to be ever better than the last. And this time
the eroticism of their surroundings had definitely helped.
Human nature in the arms of mother nature, she thought
fancifully.

Ben turned his head and smiled at her; it was a smile
of contentment, of a man who had just proved his masculinity, his virility, and proved it not only to his own
satisfaction but to that of his woman as well. A smug
smile, almost. But Nell didn't mind. On the contrary;
he'd definitely earned the right to be smug. He closed
his eyes again and she picked a blade of grass and trailed
it down his face, tickling him.

He twitched his nose and she said, 'Can you hear a tractor?'

'It's a bee.'

'As well as a bee. Listen. It's definitely a tractor—and it's coming nearer.'

'So?'

'So we don't have any clothes on, and your car is blocking the entrance to this field.'

Ben grudgingly opened one eye. 'You think we ought to move?'

'I think we ought to move. Now!'

They hastily scrambled into their clothes, the noise of the tractor's engine getting rapidly nearer, and just managed to reach the gate as it drew up in the lane. Ben apologised and quickly backed the car out of the way, then burst into laughter when he saw that Nell's cheeks were flushed red with embarrassment.

'Don't laugh!' she protested, punching him. 'He must have guessed what we were doing—your shirt's hanging out. Oh, no! And there are flowers and grass in my hair.'

'So who cares?' He suddenly caught hold of her and kissed her hard on the mouth. 'You look fantastic—and I certainly feel it. And what we did was incredibly fantastic, too. God, I can't remember the last time I made love out in the open. And in daylight, too!' He gave a laugh of pure, masculine happiness. 'Nell, you make me feel like a randy teenager all over again. I can't get enough of you. But you must know that.' He gave her an exuberant bear-hug, making her protest laughingly. 'I feel at least fifteen years younger.'

'How old would that make you?'

'About twenty.'

'Oh, dear.' She pretended to be dismayed. 'In that case I can't possibly be seen out with you again—everyone would think I'd got a toy-boy.'

He laughed, on an incredible high. 'I'll be your toy-boy any time.'

She drew back, combing the flowers out of her hair with her fingers. 'I don't want a toy-boy.'

'Then I'll be whatever you want.'

'Really?'

'Really,' he said positively.

She smiled. 'I think you'll do as you are.'

Ben's eyes softened and he bent to lightly kiss her cheek. 'That's the nicest thing anyone's said to me for a very long time,' he told her, his tone half mocking, half serious.

'Then that's something else we'll have to make up for,' she said huskily, and put her arms round his neck to kiss him. Then she drew back and lifted her hair off her neck. 'It's hot in here.'

He opened the roof and the windows, said regretfully, 'I suppose we'd better get going.' Then he glanced back at the meadow. 'I'll always remember this place, Nell—and how good it was.'

She nodded. 'I know. Our special place.'

Ben started the car, turned it and drove back towards the dual carriageway, to hurrying traffic and a world where taking time out to make love in the grass under the hot sun had now become something extraordinary, even frowned upon.

'You know,' she said dreamily as they joined the traffic stream, 'I'm beginning to think you're a romantic at heart.'

'Because I wanted to make love out in the open?'

'Have you done it often?'

'A few times. When I was at university mostly. On those summer days down by the river.'

'You see, you are romantic.'

'Not really; there was nowhere else we could go,' Ben said with a laugh.

He didn't say that he'd made love like that with his wife, she noticed. Because he hadn't, or because he didn't want to tell her? Thinking about it, Nell was glad he hadn't; she didn't want to imagine him making love as they just had with another woman.

But Ben glanced at her and said, 'How about you?'

'Oh, I didn't go to university.'

'That isn't what I meant,' he chuckled.

'I know it wasn't, but it's all you're going to get.'

They came to the first of the inevitable traffic jams and Ben was able to look at her fully. 'Why did you stipulate that we have an open relationship, Nell? Why no strings?'

'The same reason as you, I suppose,' she said lightly. 'I don't feel ready to make any commitments yet.' She shrugged. 'Maybe I never will.'

His eyes stayed on her face. 'Have you ever done so in the past?'

'Oh, you're not becoming interested in my past, are you?'

'Why shouldn't I?'

She wrinkled her nose. 'Boring.'

'Your past or the fact that I'm interested in it?'

Nell gave a small laugh. 'Both.'

The car behind honked at them and he turned back to the road. 'A career is all very good and satisfying, but it isn't enough, Nell. You have to have more out of life.'

'Now you're talking as if you're ten years older than you are,' she said coolly.

'Are you getting angry? Just because I want to know more about you? What's so terrible about your past that you won't even talk about it?'

God! Nell thought. How the hell did the conversation get round to this? Abruptly she changed the subject. 'Where do your friends live? The ones who are looking after Mark?'

Ben shot her a quizzical look but let her get away with it. 'Near Ealing. We should reach the North Circular Road soon and get to it from there.'

'You're taking me with you?' Nell said in surprise.

'Yes. That's OK, isn't it?'

'What about your friends?'

'What about them?'

'You said you told them why you wanted to leave Mark behind last night. They'll know we spent the night together.'

'Does that bother you?'

'Doesn't it bother you?' she countered.

Ben hardly thought about it before saying, 'No, it doesn't. I'm not ashamed of our being lovers. The opposite, in fact.'

Looking at him, she said softly, 'You're on a high; come down to earth.'

His eyes flicked to her and then he grinned as he looked back at the road. 'Is that what you think it is?'

'Your friends might gossip about us. Are they writers or in show business? Rumours spread like wildfire in that crowd.'

'You don't have to worry about them,' Ben assured her. 'He's an old college friend, a civil engineer, nothing to do with the business. And they'll be discreet.'

'But if you introduce me to them, if they know, then isn't that making some sort of acknowledgement that we're lovers? Won't it be a form of commitment?'

'Does that worry you?'

'You said that you didn't want to make any commitments and here you are taking the first steps already. The sex between us is great, Ben. The best. But I think it's gone to your head. That's natural after being celibate for so long, I suppose. But I think maybe it would be better if you just took me home first and then picked up Mark. Gave yourself some more time. Don't you?'

'You know, I have the strange feeling that this conversation should be reversed. Isn't it the girl who's supposed to push the man into committing himself as soon as possible?'

'You're out of date.'

He looked amused. 'Thirty-five, and already a has-been.'

'But definitely not in bed,' Nell said softly.

His mouth quirked and a triumphant light was in his eyes as he said decisively, 'We're at the North Circular, and I'm turning right—towards Ealing. We'll pick up Mark together.'

Nell had been sitting forward in her seat, half turned towards him, but now she sat back, her face tightening. 'Thanks for asking if I wanted to go,' she said shortly.

Reaching out, Ben put his hand over hers and squeezed it. 'Don't worry. Don't be afraid.'

Afraid? Was that what he thought her? But afraid of what? Of losing her independence, she supposed. Nell puzzled over it for a few minutes, then thought, What the hell? and said, 'Why do you say that? What am I supposed to be afraid of?'

Ben was silent for a moment, then he said, keeping his voice light, 'Of falling in love, perhaps.'

Her breath caught for a second, but then Nell laughed. 'Love? Now that really is a dated concept. Only moon-struck teenagers fall in love. And recover from it as quickly as possible if they have any sense.'

'I take it you're against it, then?'

'Oh, definitely. People do the most stupid things when they're in love. Why, I heard of an actress who gave up a really good part in a play, an opening she'd been working for for years, just to follow a man she was in love with to some God-forsaken place in South America. And then, after only a few months, he ditched her for some exotic dancer. She should have stuck to her career.'

'Isn't it possible to have the best of both worlds?' Ben asked mildly.

'No, men are too selfish.'

'Ouch! That was a very definite statement. I'm be-ginning to think you must have had an unhappy ex-perience some time in the past that's made you biased against men.'

He pulled into the forecourt of a garage and switched off the engine.

'I'm having an affair with *you*.' Nell pointed out quickly, filled with dismay that he should have made such an accurate guess.

Ben gave her a mock-tortured look. 'I think you're just using me. You're just out for what you can get.'

She burst into relieved laughter, then gave him a lascivious leer and ran her hands over his chest. 'I am! I am! All I want is your body.'

Ben laughed, too, but then his eyes grew serious. 'Any time. Any time you want.' And, leaning forward, he kissed her tenderly. Nell finally opened her eyes and found him smiling at her. 'I think you'd better go and get the grass out of your hair before we pick up Mark, don't you?'

She went to the ladies' room and brushed her hair, put on fresh make-up. Her clothes were rather creased but there was nothing she could do about that; at least they didn't have grass stains on them, which would have been a dead give-away. Nell looked into the mirror and sighed; she very much wished that Ben had done as she'd asked and taken her home first. There had hardly been a moment today when she had been alone, not since Ben had told her that Mark was adopted. She badly needed time to think things through, either to accept or put out of her mind the possibility that the boy might be her own son. But in her heart she knew that the latter would be impossible; the idea was in her mind and wouldn't go away until she'd proved it one way or another. But how to find out? Who to ask? And how to find the time to look into it without Ben wanting to know what she was doing? It was, she thought, all going to be terribly difficult. But maybe she could start with Ben.

When she rejoined him in the car she smiled at the glance of approval he gave her. 'No one would guess,' he assured her.

'Guess what?'

'That you're a modern-day Lady Chatterley.'

She grinned. 'Fancy yourself as the gamekeeper, huh?'

'You can make daisy-chains for me any time.'

She smiled and was silent for a while as he got back into the traffic stream, then said casually, 'Some friends of mine have been trying to adopt a a child for ages and are finding it nearly impossible. Did you have much trouble finding Mark?'

'Not too much, really. It took about a year, I suppose.'

'You were lucky, then. How did you go about it?'

Ben hesitated for a moment, then gave a small shrug and said, 'Lucy wanted a child right from the start. She desperately wanted children, to be a mother. So we found out quite early on that she couldn't have children.'

'It was something wrong with her, then? Not you?' Nell put in.

Ben nodded. 'We thought about the other methods of artificial insemination, of course, but Lucy was afraid that we might try and fail, and so have lost more time and got too old to adopt. So we decided to go ahead and adopt while we were still young.'

'Who did you go through?' Nell asked, trying to keep her voice casual. 'Was it a London agency?'

'No, a national one. Something to do with the church, I think.'

Well, that figured, Nell thought; her parents would have been bound to consider the church authorities the right people to give her child to. 'Where did Mark come from, do you know?'

'You mean which part of the country?' Ben shrugged. 'I've no idea. Lucy handled it all. Why do you ask?'

'My friends think it's more difficult for them because they live in Cornwall,' Nell lied glibly.

'Possibly they're right.'

'Do you know much about his real mother?' she asked, and waited breathlessly for him to answer.

But Ben merely said casually, 'Not a lot. She was very young, a student, I think.' He turned off the busy main road and said, 'We'll be there in a few minutes. My friend's name is Sean Peters and his wife is Jenny. They have two children, Sam and Louise.'

'The ideal family,' Nell said wryly, inwardly angry that he hadn't said anything more and that she couldn't now pursue it. 'I bet they have a dog, something big and hairy.'

Ben burst into laughter. 'Its name is Bouncer. But you'll like them. I promise.'

They turned into a tree-lined avenue of substantial houses set well back from the road, each with a drive and large front garden. Ben drove into one of them and stopped the car, turned to give her an encouraging smile. He obviously expected her to be worried about meeting his friends, but Nell had no thoughts to spare for the Peters family; all her attention was centred on Mark, because this was the first time she would see him since Ben had told her he was adopted, since she had first thought that he might be her own son.

CHAPTER SIX

THEY got out of the car and walked, not up to the front door, but through a side-gate and into the back garden, Ben with a hand on Nell's arm. She wasn't sure whether he put it there for reassurance or encouragement, but she was extremely glad of its strength and support for reasons he could never have envisaged.

As she'd guessed, the garden was large and edged with screening trees, with a deep patio which had a built-in barbecue, and there was even a small swimming-pool set in the lawn. All very moneyed middle-class. There were three children playing by the pool, making a lot of noise. Nell's eyes went to them hungrily, but she had to turn away to greet a woman who came to meet them.

'Ben! How lovely! You're in time to eat with us. We've promised the children a barbecue.'

The woman spoke to Ben but her eyes were on Nell, summing her up. As Ben's mistress, Nell realised. The girl he'd been desperate to spend the night with.

Ben went forward and kissed the woman on the cheek. 'Hello, Jenny. This is Nell Marsden. We're collaborating on the adaptation of a book.'

'Hello, Nell. So you're a writer, too? Should I know of you? Are you terribly famous?'

'Not at all,' Nell answered, shaking hands. 'I'm just a back-room hack.'

'She's being modest,' Ben said in amusement, then turned as Mark noticed him and came tearing across the

122

grass. Ben swung him up to hug him, then said, 'Hey, you're all wet! Have you had a good time?'

'Yes, but you shouldn't have gone away,' Mark answered, his arms tight round his neck.

'I had to work, old son. And I couldn't take you with me today; we had to go to a television studio.' He set Mark down, and then he said, 'Look, here's Nell. Say hello.'

Reluctantly the boy looked up at her. 'Hello, Nell,' he said obediently.

'Hi, Mark.' Somehow she said it casually, but her heart was loud in her chest and her hands were balled in tight fists at her side. She was trying to see herself in him, in his dark eyes and unformed features, looking almost for some God-given sign that he was hers. He did have brown eyes; they were the same colour as hers. And his hair was brown, too, although perhaps not as dark as her own. She tried to remember the hair colour of the boy who'd taken her virginity, but she'd so successfully shut him out of her mind that she couldn't picture him at all. She didn't want to think of him, that beast, and in a way resented having to do so. Abruptly she turned away from Mark and said to Jenny, 'Are those your children?'

Jenny called them over and then her husband came out of the house, was introduced, and asked Nell what she'd like to drink, and it all became very sociable. Everyone seemed to take it for granted that they would stay for the barbecue, and ordinarily Nell wouldn't have minded, but she so longed to be alone so that she could think. Instead she had to sit with Jenny while the men took over the cooking with the help of the children, to answer politely questions like, 'How long have you known Ben?' and, 'Do you have a family of your own?' All aimed at finding out her status, both as an indi-

vidual and with Ben. She wants to know if I'm a per-
manent fixture in Ben's life or just a passing fancy, Nell
thought, and didn't know the answer herself.

'We've known Ben for years of course,' Jenny was
saying. 'He was the best man at our wedding, and Sean
did the same for him at Ben's wedding.'

This was to let her know that they considered themselves as family almost, and that she would have to be
approved by them if she and Ben were to stay together.
But they had also been poor, dead Lucy's friends; that,
too, Nell was not very subtly made aware of. So if they
were to like her, to accept her in Lucy's place, then she
would have to pass the test: be civilised and interesting,
someone they would be pleased to invite again and could
become friends with, who could make up cosy little
foursomes or go on holiday with them and the children.
Nell could almost see the thoughts running through
Jenny's head, and wanted to run. But her work had
taught her how to be socially interesting, and being a
writer lifted her halfway there. With a small sigh, Nell
set aside her own chaotic thoughts and feelings and put
herself out to be charming to Ben's friends.

It was late before Nell finally got home that night. It
was nine-thirty before they left the barbecue, with Sean
and Jenny waving them goodbye from the doorstep,
saying that Ben must bring her again. Mark was so tired
he fell asleep in the back seat of the car, his head lolling
against the arm-rest. Glancing at him, Nell felt a great
inner urge to go and sit beside him, to put her arm round
him and hold him comfortably against her. It was such
a strong feeling that it almost frightened her. Lord, this
was no time to start feeling maternal! And why now after
all these years?

But Ben was talking to her and she had no time to analyse her feelings until Ben dropped her off and she was alone at last. Nell showered and got into bed, glad that the sheets were clean and the room tidy, glad that there was no evidence of the night of love that she and Ben had shared. Because she wanted to think straight about Mark and to leave her growing attraction and need for Ben out of it.

First; was it latent maternalism or just possessiveness that she'd felt in the car for Mark? Would she have wanted to hold him if she'd still thought of him as Ben's own son? Rationally, she didn't think that she would. She'd never felt any tendency to do so before with any other children she'd come into contact with, and she certainly hadn't felt maternal towards Mark earlier. But he was a nice little boy who'd been through a lot, so maybe it had just been compassion she'd felt. Her hunted mind latched on to the latter. Compassion was better, compassion was much safer.

The second thing she had to work out was what to do about Mark. The sensible course would be to just forget what she'd learnt, to go on as before. But all these new emotions that she'd experienced today, some of them so very strong, wouldn't listen to reason. She *had* to know the truth. Nell knew that she wouldn't have any peace until she did. And what if she found out that Mark really was her son, what then? Should she tell Ben? Tell Mark himself? What if she told Ben and he was disgusted that she'd given away her child, said he didn't want to see her again? What if he refused to let her near Mark ever again? That could be the biggest disaster of all.

What if? What if? Nell's brain went round in a whirl. But one thing emerged very clearly: she must first find out if Mark was her child. If he wasn't then all those imaginary future problems would solve themselves. And until then, until she knew for sure, she must put them out of her mind. 'Sufficient unto the day'. And what a day it had been! But immediately her next problem presented itself: how to set about finding out who Mark was. She didn't know much about these things, but thought that it wouldn't be easy. The obvious thing would be to go straight to her parents, but they were away on a long holiday to New Zealand, to visit a relative, and wouldn't be back for a couple of months. Nell didn't think she could wait that long, and wasn't sure that they would tell her anything when she did ask. They had, as far as it was possible, put the whole incident out of their minds, and they certainly wouldn't thank her for reviving it.

So where, then? The hospital where her baby had been born seemed the most likely place. But hospital records offices were most probably nine-to-five places, which meant that she would have to make an excuse to Ben and have a day off work to go to the hospital and make enquiries. Asking who had adopted one's son was hardly the kind of thing one could do over the phone, Nell thought hollowly.

She tried to think up some convincing excuse, and was still working on it when the telephone rang.

'Hello?'

'Such a questioning note in your voice,' Ben said in an amused tone. 'Do you have that many men phoning you when you're in bed?'

Nell smiled. 'I thought it might be a heavy breather.'

'If I were with you I'd hope to be breathing very heavily right now. I wish I were.'

'Oh, so do I,' she said, so sincerely that he laughed with pleasure.

But then he said, 'Are you all right, Nell? You seemed a bit subdued on the way home.'

'Why, yes, I'm fine. Just fine. Probably a bit tired, that's all. It was quite a day,' she said, more fervently than she'd intended.

'It certainly was. One of the best for a very long time.'

For a long time, she noted, but not one of *the* best, the best ever.

But Ben was going on, 'I liked waking up with you beside me, Nell. And making love to you out in the open was something else.'

'The occasional alfresco meal does make a change from eating indoors all the time, doesn't it?' Her voice was more acid than she'd intended, perhaps because of the slight jealousy her earlier thought had aroused.

Ben didn't know how to take it. He said cautiously, 'Are you really all right, Nell?'

Her tone brittle, she said, 'Yes, of course. I said so.' But then she gripped the phone tighter and gave a deep sigh. 'I'm sorry. I'm tired.'

'I'll let you go to sleep, then. Goodnight, Nell.'

'Goodnight... Ben!'

'Yes?'

'It was good for me, too. The best. And I wish you were here with me.'

She could almost hear him smile with satisfaction. 'I've an idea we're going to have to do something about that. See you at the office tomorrow, as we arranged. 'Night.'

'Goodnight.'

Nell put down the receiver, thinking that she had almost blown it. Ben had phoned for a sexy goodnight talk and she had almost let all her troubles show through. That wouldn't do. This was her problem, not Ben's. He, poor man, had enough of his own with Mark. And he was turning to her to make his life better, lighter, not to add more complications.

They were to meet at the office the next day because they had almost finished the first episode and wanted to show it to Max. Ben was there first, looking good, the tiredness gone, his shoulders no longer sagging. Nell walked into the office and he immediately took her into his arms and kissed her. Not a peck on the cheek, a full-blooded kiss.

'Phew!' When he released her Nell put her hands up to her head. 'The room's going round—or is it my senses? Where's Mark?'

'He's spending the day with Mrs Goodwin; her grand-children are coming round and she said one more wouldn't make any difference.'

'And he agreed to go?'

'No problem. He gets on really well with her grandson.' He smiled at her. 'You OK?'

'Fine.' She became businesslike and opened her bag. 'I have the disk here. I'll feed it into the machine.'

Ben raised an eyebrow, but he allowed her to draw the demarcation line, and drew up a chair to sit beside her as they worked. They made a few changes, added a few things as they read it through, but basically they were satisfied that the important first episode, with that dramatic love scene, was as they had envisaged it. They had a coffee break while it was being printed off, then took it into Max, chatted with him for a while, worked for another hour on the next episode, then grabbed some sandwiches and went out to the park to eat them.

Immediately they were out of sight of the office Ben put his arm round her waist, a gesture that shouted, This woman is mine! louder than any words. 'I told Mrs

Goodwin I might have to work late,' he told her. 'I could come round to your place on my way home.'

He said it with a certainty of acceptance that made her smile. 'I guess I could rearrange my schedule to fit you in,' she said teasingly.

'Well, thank you, ma'am.'

They sat on the grass in the park, the clouds of yesterday having melted into nothingness, leaving the sky a perfect blue again.

'This weather is too good to last,' Ben commented. He watched a young woman walking by with a baby in a pushchair and a sombre look came into his eyes. 'Sometimes I think that nothing good ever lasts.'

The woman had reminded him of his wife again, Nell realised, and wondered what it must be like to be continuously haunted by memories of grief and loss and despair. Prosaically she said, 'Of course it doesn't. Things are always changing. Think how boring and inevitable life would be if nothing changed.' She lay back on the grass. 'I sometimes think there ought to be a rule that everyone should be made to change their whole life every seven years. Their names, their homes, their partners, their careers. Pity they can't change their sex, though.'

'I think I'm hearing a sci-fi plot in the making,' Ben said in amusement.

'Do you think it could be worked up to something?'

He shrugged. 'Possibly.' Stretching out beside her, he lifted a long finger and traced her profile, lingering at her mouth. 'I hope that what we have goes on for a long time, Nell.'

She looked at him, her eyes contemplative. 'I'm good for you now, Ben. You need me. But one day you won't, and then you'll be ready to move on.'

'It isn't like that,' he answered on a positive note. 'I told you that I met other women that friends found for me, but I wasn't interested.'

'Was Jenny one of the friends?'

'Yes.'

'She won't forgive me for that.'

'She liked you a lot; she told me so. They meant it when they said I was to take you again.' Leaning forward, he lightly kissed her jawline. 'And don't try to change the subject, minx; I'm getting to recognise your evasive actions. You're special for me, Nell. Very special.' Lifting himself up on his elbow, he looked into her eyes, wide and vulnerable. 'Don't hold back, my sweet girl. Don't try and keep me at a distance.'

She gave a small laugh. 'I'm hardly doing that.'

'Physically, no, but mentally... sometimes I think you're shutting me out.'

Suddenly intense, Nell said, 'I don't always find it easy to be with men, to relax with them. But I've been more open with you than any man in my life. I—I've given you more of myself than any other man, ever.'

Ben waited for her to go on, but she quickly turned her head away, as if sorry that she'd said so much. 'Are you going to tell me why? No?' Putting his hand under her chin, he made her turn and look at him. 'It doesn't matter now. Tell me when you're ready.' He put his mouth over hers, gently kissing her lips. 'What we have is good, my darling. For me almost miraculous. I never thought I'd meet another woman who could make life worth living again. Not only that but fill it with excitement and stimulation. When I'm away from you I ache to be with you. Physically ache, deep in my stomach.'

'Oh, I *know* that feeling,' Nell said fervently. Then her eyes saddened. 'But it won't last. You should know that.'

'Not with such intensity perhaps,' Ben agreed. 'But it could develop into something even closer. It's too soon to say.'

'Into love, you mean?' He nodded but didn't speak, waiting for her to go on. 'I've never been in love,' she said on a contemplative note, then looked into his eyes. 'But you have. Is it possible to fall in love more than once?'

'Of course,' Ben answered lightly. 'It happens all the time.'

'Ah, yes, the basic reason for divorce and remarriage.' Nell sat up and looked across the park. 'Is love so very different from sexual attraction?'

'At first it's the most important part of it, I suppose, but once the first excitement wears off then it either all fades away into nothing or else grows into deeper, long-lasting feelings. I'm beginning to hope very much that it will last for us, Nell. Aren't you?'

She turned her head to look down at him, thought how great he looked. Thought also how terrible it would be if she fell in love with him but he stopped wanting her. If his feelings for her faded away but hers grew stronger. If she lost both him and Mark. This new fear clutched at her heart and she could only give him a quirky smile. 'As you said, it's too soon to say.' She glanced at her watch. 'We'd better be getting back.'

A rueful look came into Ben's eyes, but he made no comment, simply pushing himself easily to his feet to stroll along beside her.

'I'll have to take a day off this week,' Nell said as casually as possible. 'Preferably tomorrow. I've some research to do for a children's book I'm thinking of adapting.'

'Oh, which one?' Ben was immediately interested.

She'd had time to think, to look out a book that she had, in the past, thought of turning into a play. One that was set in the area where her parents had their present home. So she was able to talk of it quite easily and he wasn't in the least suspicious.

The traffic was bad that evening because of a bomb scare so they were late getting to her flat. By then Ben was so eager for her that they didn't even stop to eat before they made love. Only afterwards did Nell put together a large plate of salad and cold food which they ate like a picnic, only they had the picnic in bed. They drank champagne and fed each other grapes, told each other all the silly jokes they knew, laughed and giggled like teenagers. Again like teenagers, they touched each other a lot, too. Nell licked some spilt wine from Ben's chest, and found that he liked it so much that it was necessary to spill some more.

'This is like being on honeymoon,' Ben commented on a sigh of pleasure.

Nell grew very still for a moment, then gave a crooked smile. 'Is it?'

But Ben had noticed and immediately sat up and put his arms round her. 'Like *any* honeymoon,' he stressed. 'For any couple.'

'Of course. I know what you meant.'

But he put a hand under her chin so that she had to look into the grey eyes that held hers so steadily. 'Please don't be jealous, Nell. Believe me, you have no need to be.'

Lifting her hand, she took hold of his and opened it, then kissed his palm. 'I'm not. I'm glad you were happy. It's not that.'

'What, then?'

She gave a small shrug. 'It's difficult to say; I'm no good at describing my feelings.'

'Close your eyes and pretend you're writing,' Ben instructed.

She laughed but did as he suggested, her head leaning against his shoulder. After a few minutes, she said, 'I know it's difficult for you. I know that you must often be reminded of Lucy, especially when—we're together. I thought that eating in bed like this would be fun, but all I've done is remind you of when you were with her. And of your honeymoon, of all things.'

'Oh, Nell. My sweet girl.' Ben's arms tightened around her and he kissed her eyes so that she opened them. 'What I had with Lucy was good, almost perfect, I suppose. We shared a lot together, and of course I'm always being reminded of her. That's natural. At first it was terrible seeing her things, knowing she wasn't coming home to us. But time does make a difference. I'll always hold a place for Lucy in my heart, but I've done my grieving, Nell. I'm ready to start living again.' He smiled. 'You should know that. And please don't worry about Lucy. If I think of her then it should be my pain, not yours. I don't compare the two of you, if that's what you're worried about. And I certainly don't think of her when we're together like this.'

Putting out a finger, Nell circled his nipple, watched it harden. 'The first night we spent together,' she said slowly, 'you reached out for me in your sleep. But you called me Lucy.'

Ben swore softly under his breath. 'I'm sorry, Nell. Is that why you've been holding back from me? Are you afraid I'm still thinking about her? I'm not, I swear it.' He gave a wry grin. 'Certainly not consciously.' His eyes darkened. 'How could I when I'm with you? You're so vital, so alive.'

Not a good word to use, but he didn't notice because he'd borne her back on to the pillows and began to make love to her again, showing her in the best way he knew how that his thoughts were all for her.

Nell had gone to sleep as soon as Ben had torn himself, groaning reluctantly, away from her and gone home. The alarm clock woke her at six, she walked round to the nearby garage where she had arranged to hire a car for the day, and was soon driving out of London. At seven-thirty she stopped at a motorway restaurant for breakfast and reached her destination before nine, then had to wait for the hospital records office to open.

There was a woman on duty who wasn't at all helpful, saying she couldn't possibly look up records that were that old, and she didn't think it was allowed anyway. In the end Nell had to insist on seeing the office manager. After a longish wait she was allowed to do so—and the woman had Nell's file on her desk. Nell told her that she just wanted to be sure that her son was happy, that he was being properly cared for. She tried to be matter-of-fact, but the tension in her voice and body gave her away. The manager was kind; she looked at the file and said that the boy had definitely been given for adoption and she gave Nell the address of the adoption agency. It was associated with the church, as Nell had suspected, as Mark had been found through.

'Thank you. I'll go there,' Nell said, getting to her feet.

'Please don't expect too much. They may not be able to help you,' she was warned.

But Nell had a great feeling of confident anticipation as she drove to the county town where the adoption agency was situated. But here she came up against a blank wall. The man at the agency refused point-blank to tell her whom her son had gone to. 'I cannot give you that information,' he told her.

'But I thought people are able to find out who their real parents are nowadays.'

'Why, yes, adopted children are given the information if they decide to seek out their natural parents after they come of age. But natural *parents* are not given that right. Only the children. After all, the natural mother is given the choice of either keeping her child or of letting it go.' He glanced at the file with 'BABY MARSDEN' on the cover and took out a form. 'You signed this consent for the adoption to go ahead, Miss Marsden. And you specified that you did not wish to see the baby or meet the potential foster parents.'

Slowly Nell shook her head. 'No, I didn't sign it. My mother did.' She explained about the accident and her concussion.

'But presumably your mother was carrying out your wishes?'

'She told me my baby had died because of the accident.'

'Good heavens! Well, that is wrong certainly—but at this stage... When did you find out your child hadn't died? Did your mother tell you recently?'

It would have been so easy to say yes, to lie, but Nell couldn't. Again she shook her head. 'No, I found out from a nurse who attended the birth. I met her a couple of months later and she asked me how the baby was.'

The agent gave her a quizzical look. 'That was a long time ago, Miss Marsden, and you appear to have accepted what your mother had done. Why have you come here now? You must have some reason. You haven't just had second thoughts, now have you?'

'No.' Nell gripped her hands together in her lap. 'I heard . . . I suspect . . .' She bit her lip. 'Could you please tell me whether his mother—his foster mother, that is—could you tell me whether she's died?' The eyebrows opposite her were raised high towards a balding head. 'I was given reason to think that she might have been killed in a car crash.'

'I see. Might I ask where you had that from?' And when Nell shook her head wordlessly, 'Well, I'm sorry, Miss Marsden, but even if that had happened we might not necessarily have been informed. Only if both parents had been killed and there were no other relatives to look after the child would we be called into the case again.'

'Have you been informed? Please?' Nell begged.

But he didn't even take another look at the file. 'Even if we had I am not allowed to tell you. Too much time has elapsed since your child was adopted, Miss Marsden, for you to have any rights now. I can only advise you to forget this rumour you've heard—and to try to forget your child. It's difficult, I know, especially in your circumstances, but it's by far the best in the long run.'

'That's impossible,' Nell said, her face very pale.

'You gave your child away because you thought that he would be happy in a settled home. If misfortune has come to that home you cannot step in again and take the child away. They are his family now, and he will have to go on living with them through the good and the bad, as any normal child would.'

'I don't want to take him away,' Nell said forcefully. 'I just want to know where he is. That he's all right.'

But the man didn't believe her. He called in his secretary and told her to take Nell to another room and give her a cup of tea. 'I'm sorry I can't help you, but it's quite impossible,' he said firmly, then added in what he thought was kindness, 'Perhaps when he's old enough your son will want to find you for himself.'

Nell refused the tea and went and sat in the car, thought about her son trying to find her. God, I hope not, she thought fervently. What child would want to be told he was the result of a distasteful, drunken coupling by two teenagers after a party? Well, he might find her because her name was on the birth certificate, but he would never know his father's because she had refused point-blank to tell who it was. But what if the boy was Mark? What if *he* came looking for her? Nell thought she'd die of embarrassment if that happened. He was such a brave little boy; he deserved a whole lot better than her, than the start she'd given him.

Fighting back tears, Nell started the car and headed for the town in which she'd lived when she was at school, the place where her child's father might still be around.

Again it was a long drive, but Nell skipped lunch and got there in a couple of hours. She drove around for a while, wondering where to start. Her old house looked much the same; perhaps she could start by calling on the next-door neighbours, see if they were the same people. But they probably wouldn't be up to date with the people she'd gone to school with. Better to go to places where her contemporaries might hang out. The pubs were still open so she went from one to another, having an orange juice in each, her eyes searching the customers for a face she might recognise, but finding

none. Nor did she see anyone who looked familiar in
the new shopping precinct or any of the cafés and coffee-
shops. She was on the point of giving up and was actually driving away when she saw a group of young
mothers waiting outside a primary school for their
children to come out. Of course! Why hadn't she thought
of that before?

Nell parked the car and walked up towards the group.
Immediately she recognised two of the women who were
talking together. She made as if to walk past, did a convincing double-take, and made herself known. In no time
at all she was hearing all the gossip, the women accepting her excuse that she was looking up some old
friends of her parents. The children came out and they
all went to a nearby play area where there were swings,
a slide and a roundabout. It wasn't difficult to mention
that last, for her unforgettable party and ask what had
happened to all the boys who'd been there. Soon she
had the information she wanted; 'the beast', as she always
thought of him, was working as a trainee manager at a
supermarket in the very precinct she'd walked round.

Soon afterwards Nell said she had to get back to
London and left them looking after her with envy in
their eyes. Of them all, she, it seemed, was having the
most success out of life. Nell drove back to the precinct,
parked, and went into the supermarket. Picking up a
basket, she roamed the aisles looking for him, and was
lucky enough to hear a woman come in and complain
about some item she'd bought. A man came down to
see to her and Nell recognised the face she had hoped
never to see again. He was of average height, dark-haired,
and had skin that still showed traces of severe acne. But
was he like Mark? Nell saw no instant resemblance. There
was nothing about him that could give her the answer

she wanted, either one way or the other. Angry with herself for having come here and put herself through this, for wasting both time and emotion on it, she dropped the empty basket on the floor and walked out of the shop, strode back to the car and drove home feeling sick and empty inside.

Ben rang her that evening. 'Had a good day?'

'Yes, thanks.' She managed to keep her voice light. 'How about you?'

'I took the day off, too. I went to the British Library to do some research for my film. And guess what? I think I may have a clue to the author of *A Midwinter Night's Dream*.'

'Really?' Nell was instantly intrigued. 'Who? How?'

Ben laughed. 'I noticed in the index there was a small book of poems by a woman called Judith, Lady Tremayne.'

'J.L.T.,' Nell said excitedly. 'The same initials. Did you look at the book? Did the poems give you any clue that you might be right?'

'I haven't had time to read them all in detail, but there are a couple that would fit in very well with the story in the book. And there's something about the style of writing, even though it's verse and not prose, that suggests the same author for both. Anyway, I've borrowed the book and you can look at it for yourself tomorrow.'

'Wouldn't it be wonderful if we could find out that the story is true? Maybe we could even find the real house where they met every winter.'

Ben laughed again at the eagerness in her voice. 'It's only a guess; we'll have to do a whole lot more research before we can be sure.'

'But it's a start. How brilliant of you to spot it.'

'Can you come and work here tomorrow?' Ben asked. 'I have no one to look after Mark.'

'Yes, of course,' Nell answered at once, having expected that and come to terms with seeing Mark again.

'I've missed you today.'

'Good!'

'You're supposed to say that you missed me, too,' Ben pointed out with a chuckle.

'Goodnight, Ben.'

'Didn't you miss me one little bit?'

'Goodnight, Ben.'

'You're cruel,' he groaned. 'What have I done to deserve this treatment?'

'Goodnight, Ben.' And this time she put the phone down.

It was difficult to put her problems out of her mind, but somehow Nell managed to appear as normal as possible when she went to Ben's place the next day. Circumstances helped; Max had read through their draft and was pleased with it, wanted only a very few changes, which they worked on straight away. And Mark had a friend round, a neighbour's child, so he was in the garden the whole time and she didn't see much of him. Then there was the excitement of reading through the little book of poems during their lunch break, and immediately picking out the two poems that Ben had noticed, the first of which exactly described the feelings of a woman who had a secret lover, and the second those of grief for a lover who had died.

'I'm sure you're right,' Nell said excitedly. 'How can we find out?'

'Well, we can start with back copies of *Burke's Peerage*, she should be listed in there.'

'I'll go to the library tonight on my way home,' Nell promised.

Ben had kissed her when she arrived that day, and had done so in front of Mark, deliberately, Nell thought. But it had only been a peck of a kiss, although they managed to snatch a few hotter ones when Mark wasn't around, and he kissed her lightly again when she left— again in front of Mark, which confirmed her guess. He obviously wanted Mark to accept that they were getting close, closer than just people who were working together.

Nell didn't know how to take that. She felt terribly mixed up, her thoughts and emotions in chaos. She had been so confident that she would be able to find out the truth about Mark, and was finding it very difficult to accept that she couldn't. I should have lied, she thought bitterly, and told the man at the agency I'd only just found out he was alive. He would have told me then. Or I should have been firmer, forced him to tell me the truth. Wild ideas about breaking into the adoption agency and looking at the file came into her mind. But she remembered the big safe in the office and dismissed the idea for the fantasy it was.

That evening Nell went to the library as she'd promised. There were Tremaynes in the modern edition, but she found the entry she was looking for in a very old edition. It was for Judith, Lady Tremayne, widow of Gervase Tremayne, whom she'd married in 1860 and who had died in 1875. Two sons and two daughters. It all fitted—the length of the marriage, the number of children. Nell really felt that they were on the right track, but the library was closing and she regretfully had to leave it there.

The next day and all the following week they worked at Ben's place and got on really well with the second episode. This was mostly because the weather broke at last so Mark had to play indoors, bringing his toys into the room where they were working. He was quiet enough, often sitting for hours over a colouring-book, but they were both aware of him and were circumspect. However, Ben made a point of kissing her in front of Mark every morning and evening, and gradually let the boy see him putting his arm round her waist or on her shoulder. He tried to draw Mark in, to make it a threesome, but the boy was wary and reluctant.

Mrs Goodwin had gone on her summer holiday to Bournemouth and he had no one who would care for Mark, so Ben became extremely frustrated. They both did. In a way it was exciting; any intimacies they shared had to be snatched in odd moments when Mark was out of the room and were tantalisingly brief. Their small chaperon left them alone very seldom. It was driving Ben mad, and Nell, too, was experiencing that familiar, deep-down ache. But in some ways she wasn't altogether sorry; when she was close to Ben, held in his arms and being lifted to such glorious heights of passion, then it was virtually impossible to imagine life without him. But away from him she was able to think more clearly. About Mark, mostly, but about Ben too. And what she ought to do.

She was still half convinced that Mark was her child, nothing had changed that, but it looked as if the only way she was going to find out for sure was to come right out and ask Ben. But she shrank from doing that because she was sure it would make him change towards her. If she continued her relationship with him, in the future he might think it was only because she wanted to be near her son, not because she was in love with him. Even if she didn't ask him, Nell could envisage all sorts of problems if he ever found out. He was becoming more serious about her by the day. What if he wanted to marry her? It was his wife who hadn't been able to have children, so he was bound to want children of his own. What if she became pregnant again and a doctor asked her about her previous pregnancy? Her mind froze with horror at the thought. The adoption agency, too, had put a terrifying thought into her mind: what if she said nothing to Ben, married him, and then, when Mark was eighteen, he went in search of his real mother and found that it was her all along? Nell's mind cringed from the emotional trauma this would cause them both, especially Ben. Even eleven years of happiness before Mark came of age wouldn't compensate for that. And the dread of it happening would always be in her mind, spoiling all the good.

Despite her attraction to Ben, and feelings for him that were growing ever deeper, Nell was gradually coming to accept that she had to break with him. If there was no way she could prove that Mark was or wasn't her child without asking Ben, then she had to let him go. Let them both go. At the moment it was good for both her and Ben, but if she lied or deceived Ben over Mark, then she knew that he would never forgive her. He had experienced one perfect marriage and there was no way she could offer him less. And she had her own pride, pride that wouldn't let her deceive him so that she could be near the boy she thought was her son.

Nell took the book of poems back to the British Library, looked up older copies of *Burke's Peerage* and found the name and address of the house where Lady Tremayne had lived, but somehow the excitement had largely gone out of it now. But Ben was still curious, and suggested they go to the district and try and find the house.

'What about Mark?'

'It's Saturday tomorrow; Mrs Goodwin will be back from her holiday, and I'll ask her to look after him for two or three days next week.'

Nell looked quickly up at him. 'You mean that we'll go away together, stay somewhere?' The thought of being alone with him brought a surge of excitement and her heart began to thump in her chest.

'Yes.' Ben's hand gripped hers. 'And when we come back, I want you to move in here. I'm falling in love with you, Nell. I want you to live with me, be part of my future. My darling girl, please say you will.'

CHAPTER SEVEN

FOR a moment Nell could only gaze at Ben speechlessly, but her heart jumped crazily and she suddenly knew without any shadow of doubt that moving in with Ben was the one thing she wanted more than anything else in the world. But all the nights of torment and the reasons for them were there, too—and because of Mark love didn't completely drive out common sense. So she was able to laugh a little, albeit unsteadily, and say, 'Hey, wait a minute! If I'm not mistaken, you're the guy who only a few weeks ago said that he wasn't ready to make any commitments.'

'I know that. But that was a lifetime ago. Since then I've become sure of my feelings for you, Nell. More sure than anything in my life.'

The sincerity in his voice touched her heart, made her want to say all the things that were in it. She reached out to put a hand on his arm, but there was a noise on the stairs and Mark followed them into the kitchen where they were standing.

'Daddy, will you put the video on for me, please?'

'You know how to do it. You don't need me,' Ben answered, a note of impatience in his voice.

'Yes, I do.' Mark looked at her dourly. 'Is Nell going home soon?'

'Yes, I am,' she answered, and glanced up at the window set high in the wall. 'It looks as if it's raining; I think I'll take a taxi.'

'There's no need; I'll run you home. Mark will come with us.'

'But, Dad, I want to play my video.'

'Don't be so rude, Mark!' Ben turned angrily on the boy. 'We will take Nell home and you will be polite to her, do you understand?'

Mark nodded morosely, but his bottom lip spoke defiance. Nell sighed inwardly; it was natural that Ben had got angry, but she had been getting on quite well with Mark lately, playing games with him, talking to him, being careful not to overdo it, and she felt that he was beginning to relax with her at last. Now Ben had set that back. Not that it really mattered, she supposed, because after they'd finished this collaboration she wouldn't be seeing either of them again. But it had felt good to get even this little closer to Mark.

Ben drove her home with Mark sulking in the back, and kissed her for much longer than usual. It was Nell who broke away, said a hasty goodnight, and ran to her front door through the rain.

When Ben rang her that night, as he did every day now, he immediately asked her when she would move in with him.

'Aren't you rushing things, Ben?' she prevaricated. 'We really haven't known each other all that long.'

'Long enough for me to know that I want to be with you all the time. These last couple of weeks have been hell, seeing you every day but not being able to even kiss you properly, let alone make love to you.'

'It's just frustration, then.'

'No! It's more than that. Much more. I told you that I'm falling in love with you. I want us to be together, Nell.'

'Yes, but at your place?'

'Is that a problem?'

Slowly Nell said, 'You could have asked me to stay over at your flat any time, but you didn't because of Mark.'

'I'll talk to him, explain. He's really getting used to you being around, Nell; he'll soon be used to you being here permanently.'

'Yes, but there's another problem, isn't there?'

Ben didn't pretend not to understand. 'You mean Lucy.'

'Yes, of course. Do you really want me to take over her house? Her bed?' she added deliberately.

There was a sharp silence, then Ben said tersely, almost as if he was convincing himself, 'I'm over Lucy.'

'No hang-ups?'

'No. I want you here with me. It's—it's the only practical solution to the problem. Your place is too small for the three of us. So when will you move in?'

Having made her decision to end it, Nell realised that this was the moment when she should tell him. She opened her mouth to do so but her heart failed her. It was the first time in her life that she had really been in love, and it was such a recent discovery. It was impossible to say when instant attraction and physical desire had turned into love, but somewhere along the way it had happened and Nell just couldn't bear to end it so soon, so brutally. Surely it wouldn't be wrong to have a little more time. So instead she prevaricated, saying, 'I'm really not sure it's a good idea, Ben.'

'Why not?'

'Mark really doesn't know me all that well yet. I don't want to upset him when he's been through so much.'

'You must leave Mark to me.'

'Yes, but how is he supposed to treat me if I move in with you? As a new mother? What if it doesn't work out between us and I move out again? That will make him even more mixed up, won't it? I really don't think you're being fair on him, Ben.'

'But I need you, Nell,' Ben said forcefully. 'And Mark will soon get used to the idea; he needs some tender loving care as much as I do.'

And me, Nell thought with longing. And me. But she had to bite her lip and say, 'Look, let's not commit ourselves to any major changes. Why don't we take it gradually? I'll—I'll stay over for a night and we'll see how it works out. For both you and Mark. Take it from there.'

Ben was silent again for a moment, then he said, 'For both *me* and Mark? You think it might not work out for me?'

'Maybe you didn't ask me to stay before because you were thinking of Lucy, not of Mark.'

'I see.' Ben's voice became wry. 'You're being very practical, Nell.'

'Is that wrong?'

'Let's just say it isn't what I'd expected, or what I'd hoped, rather. I thought you'd be pleased that I wanted us to be together, that I was ready to commit myself to a lasting relationship. I didn't actually expect you to fall into my arms with joy, but...'

He paused and Nell knew that, although he'd denied it, that was exactly what he had hoped and expected she would do. Softly she said, 'I do want to be with you. You know that. It's wonderful for me, too. But I don't want to rush into anything at the cost of Mark's happiness and peace of mind. We have time, Ben; let him get used to the idea.'

'And I'm beginning to think that you need time to get used to the idea, too,' Ben said shrewdly.

'Maybe I do at that,' she admitted. 'Meeting you wasn't on the agenda.'

'I'm no danger to your career, Nell. The opposite. I'll always help you as much as I can. Surely you know that.'

'Thanks,' she said huskily, knowing that they made a good working partnership, thinking of all the projects they could do together—but the next second realising with a surge of pain that it could never be.

That night wasn't a pleasant one; as she lay sleeplessly in bed Nell would one minute decide that Mark couldn't possibly be her child, she should ignore the idea, move in with Ben and take the happiness offered to her, then the next her conscience would rear its ugly head and she would miserably accept that she dared not take the risk. Not all the happiness in the world would be worth seeing the revulsion in Ben's eyes if he ever found out, if he thought that she'd tricked him.

Next day she put all her energy into physical work: cleaning the flat, washing, ironing, baking biscuits for Ben and some special gingerbread men for Mark. And when there was no work left to do she switched to jogging and exercising until she had no strength left. Nell went to bed then, slept heavily, and when she woke in the middle of the night found that a decision had been made: she would keep up the affair with Ben, snatch what happiness she could from it and from being close to Mark, until the adaptation was finished. Then she would break with him. Try and keep his friendship if she could, if it was at all possible, but if not then let them go, say goodbye forever.

The weather had cleared overnight and the day dawned bright and warm. Nell was already up, sitting by the window that looked out over the garden, a mug of coffee in her hands, when the phone rang.

'It's us.' Ben's voice was clear and strong. 'We're taking you out for the day. Put on some casual clothes. We'll be there in twenty minutes.'

Surprise and pleasure showed in her voice as Nell said, 'Where are we going?'

'It's a surprise.'

'Shall I bring some food?'

'No, it's all taken care of. Just bring yourself.' His voice growing warm, Ben added, 'That's all we want.'

'OK, I'll be ready.'

Nell flew to dress, put on jeans and a blouse, wondered if they would be too hot and put on Bermuda shorts instead. She made-up faster than she'd known she could, threw the jeans and a sweater into a bag in case she needed them, did things unnecessarily because she was so excited. Forcing herself to stop to think, Nell realised she was behaving like some lovesick teenager. Well, that was near enough what she was. She'd never had a teenage love, she'd lost the years when girls got silly over a romance, because she'd felt so bitter, so used. It had taken a lot of years before love had finally come her way, so it was no wonder she was so exhilarated by it. So make the most of today, she told herself; make the most of every minute and remember it forever.

They went sailing. Ben hired a dinghy at a sailing club and they spent the day out on a big lake, taking it in turns to steer and mess around with the sails. It was a wonderful day, from every point of view. Mark was completely happy and relaxed, laughing as he sat with his life-jacket on and the breeze in his hair. The sun glinted on the water and the waves slapped against the side as Ben and she sat necessarily close in the small boat. And he deliberately showed no inhibitions where she was concerned, putting his arms round her and kissing her almost as much as he would have done if they'd been alone.

At lunchtime they drew into the bank for their picnic, got their feet wet as they waded ashore. After they ate Ben helped Mark to set up his fishing rod and they relaxed together on the grass a few yards away.

'I've two wonderful things to tell you,' Ben said in low-voiced eagerness. 'First, I've started preparing Mark for you moving in.'

'Oh, Ben, I haven't said that I will yet.'

'But you will,' he said with supreme confidence. 'So I told him how lonely I was and how much I liked you. I told him that I wanted to see more of you, not just while we worked, that we could all have fun together.'

'Hence today?'

'Yes.' Ben grinned. 'As a matter of fact it was Mark's idea. When I said it would be nice for us all to go out together he said one of the boys in the road was always going sailing and couldn't we go too.'

'He actually suggested it? He didn't mind me coming along?'

Leaning closer, Ben said, 'I think I laid it on pretty thickly about how lonely I was. And he must have seen that I was determined about it. Let's hope he's decided to accept you.'

Nell glanced across at where Mark sat, his body tense as he waited for the rod to bend, for a fish to bite. 'He's so very young, Ben,' she said with unknowingly deep tenderness in her eyes and voice.

'I do believe you're falling for him,' Ben said with pleasure in his voice. 'Should I be jealous? Is he the attraction and not me?' Then he frowned as she gave him a swift, startled look. 'Nell?'

Somehow she managed to laugh it off. 'Oh, I'm always on the look-out for a bargain; with you I get two men for the price of one.'

But he wasn't to be put off and took her hand. 'You seemed so surprised just now.'

'Did I?' She laughed. 'Yes, I suppose I was. I've never come into contact with a small child before.' She forced herself to say it. 'I do hope I'm not becoming maternal; that would never do.'

'Why not?'

'I'm a career-girl, remember?'

'Ah, yes, that career of yours. But even writers have been known to have children. There's nothing to prevent them.'

'You said you had two things to tell me,' Nell reminded him, desperately wanting to change the subject. 'What was the other?'

'Mrs Goodwin is back and has agreed to look after Mark so we can go and hunt down our author. She'll move into my flat while I'm away and will stay for two nights. Two nights, Nell!' He gripped her hand tightly, his eyes darkening at the mere thought of making love to her again, of two whole nights of love.

Nell's lips parted and her breath caught as she, too, thought what it would mean. 'Oh, Ben,' she breathed. 'When? When can we go?'

'Tuesday morning. She'll come round at nine and I'll drive over and collect you. We needn't come back until Thursday afternoon. Mrs Goodwin goes to her Women's Institute meeting on Thursday evening so we have to be back in time for her to go home and get ready.' He gazed into Nell's happy, excited eyes. 'Oh, Nell, my sweet, I can't wait to be alone with you again, to take you to bed.'

'Dad! Dad, I think I've caught something.'

Mark's excited shout brought Ben to his feet to go and help. He gave Nell a rueful smile, but the happiness of anticipation was still in his eyes, his face.

Thank God I didn't break it off yet, Nell thought. At least I'll have a few precious days to look back on. And I'll make them good, because it looks as though they're going to have to last me a lifetime.

On Tuesday morning Nell was ready much too early, eagerly waiting for Ben to arrive. When he did he swept her into his arms to kiss her and would have made love to her there and then if she hadn't laughingly stopped him.

'No! You've got to wait till tonight.'

'I can't. I want you now,' he muttered as he kissed her throat, her eyes, then returning ragingly to her lips.

Putting her hands against his chest, Nell held him off. 'But I want to wait until tonight.'

'Why? Why not now? We have time.'

'But we'll have more time tonight. And we'll have the whole day knowing that we're going to make love,' she said softly. Gently running her fingertips down either side of his face, she went on, 'We'll have dinner and take our time over our coffee, then we'll go up to our room and we'll very slowly undress one another.' She kissed his lips lightly, sensuously. 'And then we'll make love very, very slowly, because we'll have all the time in the world. The whole night.' She stood back and smiled at him. 'Isn't that a better prospect than rushing into bed now?'

Ben groaned. 'It's been two whole weeks, Nell.'

She laughed teasingly. 'Then another day won't hurt you.'

But he caught her arm and said, his voice tense, 'If you only knew how much I want you.'

Suddenly serious herself, she said, 'Do you really think I don't know, that I don't feel the same? But I want to wait. I want tonight to be perfect for us.'

'Every time I make love to you is perfect,' Ben said with deep sincerity.

Nell laughed at him and returned a light answer, not wanting them to get too serious, but there were misty tears in her eyes as she got into the car.

They drove up to Derbyshire, along a route that covered the backbone of the country and took them to the heart of England, from the rolling patchwork of cultivated fields in the south to the open moorlands of the Midlands. The address Nell had found, Furstenbury Hall, proved to be a house set in its own large grounds, situated in a still unspoilt valley. There were high wrought-iron gates at the entrance that were firmly closed. Nell and Ben stood outside them, peering in, just able to see the house in the distance.

'It looks right,' Nell remarked. 'The same period as she described in the book.' She pointed excitedly. 'And look, isn't that a copper beech on the lawn to the left of the house? Do you remember how Anna used to go and sit under it when she wanted to be alone and think about her lover? We must be right. This must be the place.'

'It certainly seems like it,' Ben agreed.

Nell reached to open the great latch on the gate. 'Let's go in and enquire.'

But Ben said, 'I think we'd better make as certain as we can first. Let's go to the local records office and see if we can find anything about the Tremaynes. And we'd better find out who lives here now.'

So they went to the nearest town, found the archives office, and with the help of an interested assistant got the information they were looking for.

'The house still belongs to a member of the Tremayne family,' the girl told them. 'Only the main branch died out and it went through the female line and now belongs to a Mrs Westmacott. She's quite a nice old lady. Lets the local History Society hold their summer party in the grounds. And she does a lot of work for charity, too. I'm sure she'd be pleased to help you.'

'Do you know her yourself?' Ben asked.

'Oh, yes. I'm the secretary of the History Society, you see.'

Ben gave her one of his most winning smiles. 'Then I wonder if you would be very kind and phone her for us? Explain that we're bona fide researchers and would be very grateful if we could call to see her.'

The assistant found the smile irresistible and went off to do as he asked.

Nell shook her head at him. 'And they say women use their wiles to get their own way.'

Ben grinned. 'I'm merely practising for tonight.'

'It will take more than a smile.'

'I intend to give you more than a smile.'

He bent to kiss her but she drew back. 'Oh, no. I may just punish you for flirting with other women.'

But Ben put a hand behind her neck and held her while he gave her a very businesslike kiss, then hastily let her go as he heard the assistant returning. Nell blushed and had to turn away, could only murmur a garbled thank-you as the girl told them Mrs Westmacott would be happy to see them if they'd like to go straight away.

Outside the office Ben burst into laughter. 'You should see your face!'

'She might have caught us. I'm not used to being kissed in public.'

Ben put his arm round her waist. 'It's your own fault for being so beautiful—and for saying no this morning. Why don't we find a nice, empty meadow?' he cajoled. 'Remember how good it was the last time?'

As if she could forget. But Nell resisted the temptation. 'No, we have to go and see Mrs Westmacott. That is why we came here, after all.'

'It wasn't the main reason I came—and you should know that.'

'Should I?' She gave him a flirtatious look. 'Tell me about it tonight.'

Nell had imagined Mrs Westmacott as being a little, elegant old lady, but she turned out to be plump and jolly. She gave them coffee in a beautiful room full of Georgian furniture and said, 'I hear you're interested in a member of my family?'

'Yes. The Lady Tremayne we're researching lived in the house around the last half of the nineteenth century. And she was the daughter of a family who lived in Doncaster, the Peverills,' Ben explained.

'And why are you so interested in her?'

'Nell—Miss Marsden—came across this book.' He opened his briefcase, took out the book and handed it to her. 'Nell tried to find out who the author was but it hadn't been registered with the British Library, so we thought it might have been self-published. Then I happened to come across a book of poems by Judith, Lady Tremayne, and we wondered if it could be the same person.'

Mrs Westmacott looked at the book, then gave it back to Ben. 'That hasn't explained your interest.'

'I'm a writer, Mrs Westmacott,' Nell told her. 'I adapt books for radio plays and serials. When I came across *A Midwinter Night's Dream* I immediately thought that it lent itself for adaptation—but for television rather than radio. I took the book to a producer and he agreed with me and commissioned Ben and me to adapt it.'

'I see.' The older woman paused. 'Of course the book is rather... shall we say... salacious?'

'No, I wouldn't say that at all,' Nell answered immediately. 'I think it's romantic. One of the most romantic books I've ever read. And that's how we want the concept to come across. We're not out to make a sex-ridden series, we're out to tell a romantic story.'

Mrs Westmacott looked at her earnest face for a long moment, then stood up. 'Come with me.'

She led them from the room, across the broad hallway and into a library that overlooked the grounds at the back of the house. Going to a shelf, she took down the identical book, but one that was in almost pristine condition. Then she went to a drawer, looked through some files and took one out. She laid the contents on a big table beneath one of the windows and sorted out an envelope. 'Here are the letters between Lady Tremayne and the company that printed the book.'

Ben immediately sat down and began to go through the letters but Nell lifted excited eyes to Mrs Westmacott. 'So she *did* write it. And this is the house she described, with the copper beech where she used to go and sit.'

'Yes, indeed. As far as I am aware, she was the only one of my ancestors to have written a book.'

Nell put her hand on Ben's shoulder. He glanced at her, then said, 'Which leaves one very interesting question, Mrs Westmacott. Is the book a work of fiction—or was it true? Did Lady Tremayne have a secret lover who turned out to be her own husband, or did she make up the whole thing?'

'Ah. Now that I'm not so sure about,' the old lady told them. 'You see, Lady Tremayne's grandson, the one who inherited this house, had very Victorian values. He wasn't at all pleased to think that one of his ancestors had written such a passionate book. There were several copies of it here then, but he ordered them all to be burnt. But luckily his sister, who is *my* ancestor, managed to save one of them—the book you're holding. Unfortunately he also destroyed Lady Tremayne's diary which would have told us whether it was true or not.'

'But surely his destroying the diary points to it being her own story,' Nell said quickly.

'I've always thought so,' Mrs Westmacott agreed with a smile. 'But unfortunately it's more difficult to prove. However——' she crossed to another chest of wide drawers '—I have here some documents which state that her husband purchased a much smaller house near Alfreton, some three years after their marriage. It's about two hours from here if you travelled by horse and carriage, and it's close to the old road you would have to take if you were travelling here from Doncaster.' She gave a twinkling smile as she saw the delighted amazement in their faces. 'Oh, yes, when I read the book I was as interested to find out if it was true as you are. The story absolutely fascinated me. So I did some research of my own, and I'm as sure as I can be that it really happened.'

'This is marvellous!' Ben exclaimed. 'But—would you have any objections to our adapting it for television? After all, she is your ancestor and——'

'Good heavens, no!' Mrs Westmacott broke in. 'I love television. It keeps me happy for hours when I'm here alone. And some of the book adaptations have been superb. Did you see *Clarissa*? And then there was the *Eastern Trilogy*——' She broke off as they both smiled.

'Ben did that adaptation,' Nell said, an unconscious note of pride in her voice.

'Did you? I did enjoy it. And now I'm quite sure that Judith's story is in good hands. Would you want to say that it's based on a true story? Yes, I suppose you would. Although I would, of course, prefer that you didn't mention the name Tremayne, or my name or the name of this house.'

'Of course not,' Ben assured her.

'Good. Then I shall look forward to seeing it.'

She glanced at her watch and Ben said quickly, 'We've taken up too much of your time.'

'Not at all. I was just going to ask you if you'd care to stay to lunch. I should be so interested to hear about your work.'

Mrs Westmacott had been so kind that it would have been impossible to refuse, but they wanted to stay anyway. They were both so excited at having their hopes confirmed that they couldn't stop talking about it and wanted to hear any detail that the old lady could tell them.

It was well into the afternoon before they left, each of them having made a friend. 'Oh, there's just one thing,' Ben said as they stood in the hall to say goodbye. 'You haven't given us the exact address of the house where they met. Do you still own it?'

'I'm afraid not. Lady Tremayne's grandson sold it.'

'That's a shame. But we'd like to go there tomorrow and take a look at the house, if we can get permission from the present owners.'

'Oh, I don't think you'll have any trouble getting permission, but I'm afraid you won't get much of the original atmosphere from it. You see, the place has been turned into one of those country house hotels that are so popular nowadays. It's called Goldenhill Hotel.'

'Thank you. You've been very kind,' Ben said with sincerity.

'Not at all. What an enjoyable visit. Do come again whenever you're near, won't you?' She smiled at them. 'And good luck to you both in your future together.'

When they got outside and into the car, Ben said with a big grin, 'Well, at least there's one person who thinks we have a future together.'

'She's a romantic,' Nell returned. 'A sucker for a good love story. And thank heavens she is. We might never have found out the story is true if it hadn't been for her romantic nature.'

'Speaking of a romantic nature,' Ben said as they drove away, 'and having one myself, how about if we try to book a room for tonight at the Goldenhill hotel?'

'Oh, yes, *please*.' Nell turned to him with delight in her face. 'That would be a really fitting climax to today. And do you think, would it be at all possible——?'

'To have the room where the two of them made love?' Ben finished for her. Reaching out, he put his hand over hers. 'You shall have it, my darling, if I have to throw the present guests out with my own hands.'

It didn't come to that. When they reached Goldenhill they walked round the outside of the house first, found the group of trees and the gazebo that Lady Tremayne had described looking out on from the bedroom window, and so were able to pin-point the room. Then they went into the hotel and Ben, acting to the manner born, told the receptionist that they were on a second honeymoon and wanted to stay in the room where they had spent their first. 'Just for two nights,' he said persuasively, and making use of the smile. 'Unfortunately that's all we can spare away from our son.'

He had said it only to emphasise his story, but just to hear Mark described as her son gave Nell a jolt. Today had been so extraordinary, and knowing that she and Ben were going to be together tonight so wonderful, that she had almost forgotten all her problems and the harrowing decision she'd taken. But now it all came back, and seeing Ben, having secured the room, sign the register as Mr and Mrs Rigby didn't help.

When he turned towards her, laughing triumph in his eyes, he met a coolness in her face that startled him. 'Nell?'

But she looked away and left him to go out to the car to get their cases alone.

By the time he came back she'd had time to recover a little and realise that she mustn't let anything spoil today. So she gave him a bright smile when he asked her what was the matter and said, 'It was nothing. Just someone walking over my grave, that's all.'

'Don't say that! Don't ever say that,' Ben said sharply.

'What? Oh! Oh, Ben, I'm sorry. I didn't think.'

'No...' He gave a rueful shake of his head. 'I'm sorry. You shouldn't have to be sensitive about it.' Deliberately changing the subject, he said, 'Do you recognise any of this from Lady Tremayne's description?'

Gladly following his lead, Nell looked around. 'The arched doorways are the same. And yes! She described the staircase as having newels carved as unicorns holding shields.' She went over to touch one of the wooden beasts reverently, looked round the hall, trying to imagine it as it must have looked on that long-ago wintry night.

A porter came to take their cases and they followed him up the staircase and along the first-floor corridor to the bedroom. Nell walked into the room and gasped in awe. The room was dominated by a huge four-poster bed. Her face animated, she turned to the porter. 'How long has this bed been in this room? Is it a new one— new to the house, I mean?'

'Oh, no, madam. The present owners inherited the house and all the furniture in it.'

'Really? When was that?' Ben asked.

'About fifteen years ago, I think. But the place was too big for them so they decided to turn it into a small hotel. I'm sure they'd be pleased to tell you all about the history of the house, if you're interested, sir.'

'Thanks. We'd like to meet them.' Ben gave the man a tip, was thanked, and the porter went out and shut the door behind him. Ben turned to Nell, said, 'Come here,' in a tone that wasn't to be denied, and took her into his arms.

He kissed her thoroughly, as a woman ought to be kissed, holding her close against him and bending her to his body. His mouth was firm and his kiss deep and demanding. It was a kiss both of possessiveness and promise, a reminder of the times they'd been together and in anticipation of the night that was to come.

Nell reeled a little when he finally let her go, making Ben laugh softly. 'It was you who wanted to wait till tonight,' he pointed out.

She wrinkled her nose at him, then turned to have another look round the room. 'The curtains on the bed must be different. Lady Tremayne said they were made of thick velvet in a rich-red colour. That it was impossible to see even the glow of a candle through them. But this looks like a Laura Ashley print.' She went to the bed and fingered the material, a pattern of small flower clusters on a light background.

'The original hangings probably fell apart with age. And they'd have had to redecorate the room when they turned it into a hotel.' Ben opened a door off to the left. 'And this room, which she described as a dressing-room, is now a very modern bathroom.'

'But the view is the same.' Going to the window, Nell raised the sash window and looked out. 'Look. There's the gazebo and the trees. And you can just see the church spire in the distance.' She gave a contented sigh and looked round the room. 'Just think how many people must have stayed in this room since it became a hotel, and yet none of them knew its secret. Only us. Shall we tell the owners, do you think?'

'Possibly when we leave.' Ben came to put his arms round her waist. 'Max might want to use this house for his location shots.'

'And Furstenbury? Mrs Westmacott would like that, I think.'

'Yes, I'm sure she would.' He kissed her neck, put a hand up to unbutton her blouse.

But Nell firmly pushed him away. 'I think it's about time to get ready for dinner.'

Ben sighed. 'I'm beginning to think you're a tease, sweet Nell.'

Ben took the opportunity to ring Mrs Goodwin to check on Mark, and spoke to them both, laughing at something Mark said and promising to bring him back a present. They took it in turn to use the bathroom and change, Ben putting on a suit and Nell a beautiful dress in amber silk that she hadn't worn before. They looked good together, Nell thought, except that she wished, as always, that she were taller. Especially when she was with Ben; he seemed even taller when he wore a dark suit. But then, if she'd been tall and blonde and willowy Ben might not be with her now, Nell thought prosaically.

There was a bar off the hallway that they worked out must have been a bookroom in Lady Tremayne's time. Here they met the proprietor who was doubling as the barman, and were soon chatting to him about the history of the house.

'Yes, it's been in my family for almost a hundred years now,' he told them. 'And I understand that my great-grandfather bought it complete with all the furniture, so, yes, the bed in your room has always been in the house.'

Somehow this was the last detail that made the day complete, perfect. They ate dinner in the room that looked just as a Georgian dining-room ought to look, with draped curtains and candles in wall-sconces, with polished tables and crystal glasses that reflected the light. They drank wine and toasted each other across roses in a silver bowl, touched hands and thought only of each other, only distantly aware of the waiter that came and went, of the other diners and the discreet hum of talk and laughter.

After dinner they followed the others into the drawing-room for coffee, sat on a window-seat and watched the sunset, the flaming reds and pinks promising yet another beautiful day tomorrow. When the sun finally sank over the horizon, Ben reached out and took her hand. Nell turned to look at him, saw the intense desire in his eyes and felt her own heart overflow with love for him, swell until she thought her chest too small to contain it. She swallowed, tried to speak but couldn't. But there was no need for words—her eyes said it all.

Ben got to his feet, her hand still in his, murmured goodnight to the other guests, and drew her after him into the hallway. They looked at the staircase and thought of those other, secret lovers as they ascended it. They came to their own room, lit by moonlight from the uncurtained window, and looking so much as it must have done all those long years ago. It lent the room a haunting atmosphere, but in the warmest sense of the word. Nell thought that any ghosts that were here would thoroughly approve of them tonight. Ben didn't turn on the light, immediately realising and falling in with her mood.

Nell went to the four-poster and ran her hands over the carved wood, wondering if those other hands had done the same, had touched just this spot. Going to the window, she opened it and leaned her arms on the sill, looking out. Ben had stayed by the door, watching her, but now he came over and stood behind her as he put his hands on her waist and bent to kiss her neck. He did so unhurriedly, his lips soft, languorous, but sensual enough to make Nell sigh in contentment, to tilt her head back so that he could kiss her throat. Ben's hand went to the zip of her dress, drew it slowly down, and, still standing behind her, he gently took off the rest of her clothes.

His hands on her warm skin were cool, cool as the soft breeze that came from the window. And his fingers were just as light, feathering over her breasts, tantalising the nipples until they stood proud and erect, beating the softest tattoo on the flat plane of her stomach, and touching, as lightly as a butterfly, the low warmth of her femininity. He withdrew for a few moments, there was the rustle of clothes, and then he was back, his hands caressing her again. But this time he held her against him and she could feel the heat of his naked body against her skin, the hardness of his muscles and the strength of his legs. The soft dew of scarcely controlled anticipation mingled with her own, and the growing hardness of his body let her know how much he wanted her. But still Ben caressed her, his hands cupping her breasts, his kisses on her throat and shoulders making her moan and pant with desire. She moved voluptuously, wanting him, needing him, and he gasped, his body quivering. His hands began to tremble but still he fondled and caressed her. Nell could stand it no longer. She gave a cry and turned in his arms, flung her own round his neck and kissed him with desperate, uncontrollable need.

It was what he had been waiting for. Ben swung her up into his arms and carried her to the four-poster. He dropped her on to it and moved over her, looked down at her avid, desire-racked face for a triumphant moment, and then took her in a rage of passion that was primeval in its intense urgency and yet was an unselfish sharing of love and pleasure that seemed to last forever.

When it was over, when Nell had recovered and Ben had fallen asleep beside her, she lay in the great bed and looked round the room, thought of Lady Tremayne and the pleasure her secret lover had given to her in this very bed. Perhaps their spirits had been here tonight, she thought fancifully, encouraging them, lifting them both to such dizzy heights of passion. Because tonight had been perfect for both of them. There could never, she was sure, be anything better than this. Nell felt as if her whole life had led up to this moment, as if she'd always been waiting for it, and now she had the moment of her life that she would always remember.

'To have and to hold'. The words, part of the wedding ceremony, came strangely into her mind, strangely when she would never hear them spoken in their true context. But it was almost as if her thought had reached Ben's subconscious. He stirred, awoke, and turned to take her in his arms. 'My darling Nell,' he said softly as he kissed her. 'You've made life wonderful for me again. I love you so much. Say you'll marry me, my love. Please say yes.'

There were tears in Nell's eyes as she returned his kiss, but she didn't say anything, just roused him until they were making love again. Perhaps he took her silence for acceptance, because Ben smiled as he fell asleep again. Twice more in the night they made love, and each time was exquisite, but when Ben woke in the morning, when the sun sent golden rays across the four-poster, he found that she was gone.

CHAPTER EIGHT

BEN found Nell down in the garden, sitting in the gazebo. She had been gazing into space but when she saw him coming picked up a newspaper and pretended to be reading it.

'Good morning.' Sitting down beside her, he pulled the paper down and bent to kiss her.

It would have been a deep kiss but after only a couple of seconds Nell pulled away and said, 'Have you seen this article in the paper? The government have given the go-ahead for the new television channel. There should be some work there for anyone who gets in quickly. I have some friends who——'

'Don't talk about work,' Ben commanded. 'Let's talk about us.' He put his arm round her and nuzzled her neck, gently kissing her ear.

But she pulled away. 'That tickles.'

Ben laughed. 'So I've found your weakness, have I?' His eyes grew serious, loving. 'Last night was incredibly wonderful, Nell. The best.'

She raised an eyebrow and said, with deliberate cruelty, 'Better than with your wife?'

Ben's eyes hardly flickered. 'Yes,' he answered simply.

That one word and the way he looked at her when he said it almost overcame Nell, but she had a part to play so she gave him a brittle smile and said, 'I bet you say that to all your mistresses!'

He frowned, then took her hand. 'I wasn't just saying it last night, Nell,' he said earnestly. 'I meant it. I love you and I want you to marry me.'

Withdrawing her hand, she stood up and walked out of the gazebo into the garden. 'They don't have a swimming-pool or anything here; there's nothing to do. Now that we've found out that the story is true and this is the house where Lady Tremayne met her lover, we might as well go back to London. We've got what we came for.'

She went to walk back towards the house, but Ben caught her wrist and swung her round to face him. 'Nell? What's the matter with you this morning?'

'Nothing.' She turned her head away. 'It's boring here, that's all.'

'Boring!' He stared at her averted face. 'And was last night boring, too?'

She shrugged. 'It was OK.'

'*OK*? My God, the most wonderful night of my life, and all you can say is that it was OK! What the hell's the matter with you, Nell?'

Pulling her wrist free, she rounded on him angrily. 'Look, we spent the night together, so what? It's no big deal. Do you have to keep on about it?'

'Yes. I do.' Putting his hands on her arms, Ben gazed into her face searchingly, his own eyes full of angry amazement. 'Something's happened to you, I know it has. Yesterday you were as eager for us to be together as I was. You were caught up in the magic of that room.'

'There was no magic,' Nell broke in. 'It was just a room and a bed. And all we did was to have sex. Now you want to turn it into a big love scene.'

Ben's eyes widened incredulously. 'Is *that* why you're behaving in this crazy way—because I told you I love

you? Because I asked you to marry me?' He gave a dis-
believing laugh. 'It is, isn't it?'

'We were going along fine. Why did you have to get
heavy? We both agreed no strings.'

'That was at first, before we found out we loved each
other.'

'No, you mean before you mistook sex for emotion
and *decided* we loved each other. As far as I'm concerned it was just satisfying sex; love didn't come into
it,' Nell told him, her face hard and set but her heart
crying inside.

But Ben gave her an angry shake and said, 'I don't
believe you. No one could have responded the way you
did last night and not be in love.'

'Rubbish! I'd respond that way with any man I was
in bed with.'

The words hit him like a blow, made him freeze into
stunned silence. For a long moment he was too shocked
to move, but then Ben's fingers suddenly dug fiercely
into her arms, making her give a small cry. 'How *dare*
you say that to me? Why are you doing this? You know
you don't mean it. I'll never believe you mean it.'

Nell tried to deny it again but found she couldn't.
Instead she petulantly shook him off and began to walk
back to the house, saying, 'I'm going home.'

But Ben angrily came to stand in front of her,
spreading his arms so she couldn't get by. 'We're booked
in here for two nights.'

'You can tell them we have to leave, think of an
excuse.'

'And just what shall I tell them?' he demanded bitterly. 'That you've suddenly decided we're
incompatible?'

The raw hurt in his voice made her flush, but there was no going back now. Nell bunched her hands into tight fists and said, 'Oh, tell them anything you like! I don't care.'

But his intent eyes had caught the momentary lapse, and Ben said tensely, 'But maybe you do at that. You're doing this for a reason, Nell, deliberately trying to make me angry. And I'm not going to let you go until you tell me why.'

Cursing herself, Nell tried to bluster it out. 'This is ridiculous! You're behaving like a chauvinist pig. Let me by.'

'Not until you give me an explanation. You owe me that.'

She drew herself up, her eyes darting fire. 'I don't owe you a thing! If I want to finish it, then that's my decision. I don't have to——'

'Finish it?' Ben stared at her in disbelief. 'After last night you can talk about splitting up?' He gasped and shook his head in open-mouthed amazement. 'Just what is it with you?'

Realising that Ben was getting really angry and frustrated, Nell tried to be a little more conciliatory. Spreading her hands, she said, 'Look, we don't have to talk about this now. Have you eaten? Let's go and have some breakfast.'

'No! We're going to sort this out here and now. You just tell me what the hell is going on.'

'All right. You don't have to shout.' Biting the inside of her lip, Nell took a deep breath and turned away from him as she said, 'I don't want to go with you any more. I want to end it.'

Reaching out, Ben put his hand on her shoulder and jerked her round to face him. His face dark with unsuppressed fury, he said grittingly, 'Look at me while you destroy my life again, can't you?'

She winced, but Nell's chin came up. 'You heard me.'

'And just why have you decided this is the moment to split?'

'I told you; you got too serious. I don't want to marry you or move in with you.' Her voice faltered for a second but then she forced herself to say the most cruel thing of all. 'I don't love you. But even if I did, I wouldn't want to go on with it. Your life is too complicated. I don't want to have to watch what I say and do all the time in case I remind you of your wife. I don't want to live in the house that was yours and hers and see her picture on the wall and make love in the same bed you made love to her in. And—and most of all I don't want to take on a child that isn't mine and who resents me all the time. My life is OK as it is. Sex with you was OK, it was good, but—but that's all I ever wanted from you.'

Nell stopped, and could barely lift her eyes to look at Ben. She had known how his face would look, his dear face, known that it would be full of anger, but she could never have guessed how deeply she had hurt him, how his eyes had closed tight against it, his jaw thrust forward and his hands clenched into balled fists, the knuckles showing white. He didn't speak, but suddenly turned from her with a violent movement of repulsion and strode away, not towards the house but across the garden and through the trees.

Nell's shoulders sagged, the strength that had helped her play the part suddenly gone. She sank down on the grass and put her head in her hands, completely spent now that it was over. But it had had to be done. For both their sakes, for Ben's and Mark's. As for herself nothing mattered except that Ben would have a chance now to find someone else to love, to be Mark's new mother, someone with whom they could be happy and with no fear of their lives being disrupted at some future date. It had been the only way, to do it like this, before it became too intense. Although she had left it almost too late, her longing for this one more night together had been utterly selfish, and it had made Ben tell her he loved her, which she'd been hoping to avoid. It would have been better if she'd made the break before this, then maybe they could have stayed friends, but now she'd had to make him hate her and make the break final.

The sun had come out fully and was hot on the back of her head. Nell stayed where she was for a few minutes, then realised that Ben mustn't find her here in case he guessed the truth, so she hauled herself to her feet and went back to the house and to their room. The bed was still tumbled, the clothes they'd worn last night thrown on to the chair where Ben had tossed them in his panting eagerness. Methodically, Nell found her case and packed her things tidily into it, her mother's training too deeply ingrained even for her to ignore it at a time like this when all she wanted to do was to run as far and as fast as she could.

She put on some make-up to cover the whiteness of her face and had just picked up the telephone to ask for a taxi when Ben came into the room. His face was set rock-hard but he had himself well in check now. One glance took in her packed case and the telephone in her hand. 'Are you ordering breakfast?' he asked coldly.

'No, a taxi to the nearest station.'

'That won't be necessary. When I've had breakfast I'll take you back to London.'

'You don't have to do that. I can easily——'

'I brought you here and I'll damn well take you back!' For a moment Ben's rage erupted, frightening her into silence.

Then Nell said carefully, 'Yes, all right. Shall I order breakfast in here?'

'No, I'll eat in the dining-room.'

'Shall I come with you?'

He gave a short, bitter laugh. 'Do as you like.'

So they went downstairs together and sat opposite each other at the table. It was the usual buffet arrangement where everybody helped themselves and they only had to look bright and normal when the waitress asked them whether they wanted tea or coffee. They ate in silence, Nell finding herself completely unnerved by Ben's controlled coldness, wishing now that she'd hurried and left before he came back.

After breakfast he went to Reception, explained that they had to leave early, and paid the bill. In no time at all they were in the car and heading away from the hotel. As they left, Nell turned to look back, holding the picture of the house in her mind, knowing that she would never forget last night, but ruefully wishing that she could forget this morning.

They had little to say to each other on the way back. Ben asked her to look at the map and give him directions, and once they stopped for petrol, but they had a good run and were back in London before lunchtime.

Ben drove straight to Nell's flat and got out of the car to take her case out of the boot.

'Thanks.' She stood on the pavement not knowing quite what to say, her eyes lowered. 'I'll tell Max that I'm pulling out of the collaboration, that you'll finish it alone.' She gave a small smile. 'You never really needed me anyway.'

'Don't be ridiculous!' Ben snapped. 'You signed a contract to do all three episodes. It won't do your precious career any good if you start breaking contracts for no reason. You'll be at my place tomorrow morning, as usual.'

'No, I can't do that!' She raised hunted eyes to meet his, than had to look quickly away again.

'Why?' Ben asked derisively. 'Don't tell me you'd feel uncomfortable working with someone you'd just kicked in the teeth? But that's hardly your scene, is it? You don't care who the hell you hurt!'

'That isn't true,' Nell said stiffly. 'I broke it off before we got too involved.'

'Before *you* got too involved, you mean,' Ben said shortly. He got back in the car. 'Till tomorrow. Nine o'clock sharp.'

Nell watched him drive away—and suddenly found that there were tears pouring down her cheeks. It seemed to take ages to find her key and fumble it into the lock. Her case was abandoned in the hallway as she ran upstairs and threw herself on to her bed, giving way at last to misery and tears.

Later, much later when there were no tears left, she washed her face and phoned Max. As brightly as possible she said, 'Hi, Max. How are you? Yes, I'm fine, thanks. I'm glad you liked the first episode of the serial. It's really going the way I envisaged it. Ben's really good. In fact he doesn't really need me. And I've been offered this new project, so I wondered if—— '

She broke off to listen as Max demanded to know what was wrong.

'No, there's nothing wrong, it's all going along marvellously. As a matter of fact we found out that the story is true, and we've found the houses where the author lived.' Briefly, she explained, then, 'Yes. Yes, Ben did go with me. Look, Max, I really would like to leave the project now and——'

But Max wouldn't hear of it and insisted she finish the script. Nell sighed, but agreed that she would. She hadn't really been very hopeful of getting out of the contract, but felt that she had to try. But she was dreading having to face Ben tomorrow. She should never have agreed to go away with him, and they should never have spent last night together. She had abandoned herself to love, to the wonder of it, and Ben, too, had been so moved that he'd told her he loved her. But then her self-ishness had precipitated the dreadful tension she had hoped to avoid.

It was Mark who came to open the door to her the next morning. He greeted her with a big smile and told her Ben was down in the kitchen. 'We're making some popcorn.' He took her hand. 'Come and watch. It's really good when it all bangs about in the pan.'

He had never greeted her so naturally before, had never been so friendly. Nell's heart caught and she let him lead her down to the kitchen where Ben was standing by the stove. He was wearing a T-shirt and shorts with a plastic apron over them. He glanced up at her, said a coolly casual good morning, but his eyes lingered on her face, noting the smudges of sleeplessness around her eyes that make-up couldn't hide.

'Would you like some popcorn, Nell?' Mark asked her.

She was touched, not only by the offer, but because he'd spontaneously used her name, which he didn't often do. 'Yes, please, if there's enough.'

'There's loads, isn't there, Dad?'

'Plenty for everybody,' Ben agreed. He took the pan from the cooker. 'Sounds as if it's done now. Here, you and Nell hold this big dish and I'll pour it in.'

So, willy-nilly, Nell found herself helping and listening to Mark as he told her that his friends were coming round to play with him. 'We're playing spacemen,' he told her. He glanced at his father. 'Can I tell her, Dad?'

Ben shrugged. 'Sure, go ahead.'

'Tell me what?'

Mark turned a glowing face up to her. 'We're going to the seaside.'

'Are you? For a holiday?' Nell asked, unable to keep the relief out of her voice. 'How wonderful. When are you going?'

'On Saturday. But it's not a holiday, it's for the weekend. We're going to go sailing again. Aunty Jenny has invited us. She has a cottage at the seaside. It's really good there.' Mark grinned at her, displaying a gap where a baby tooth had fallen out. 'And you're coming, too. She said we had to bring you.'

'Me? Oh, but——'

Ben's voice cut incisively through her refusal. 'You're coming with us.' He gave her a gritty look and said with smiling sarcasm that was lost on Mark, 'The weekend wouldn't be the same without you.'

'Yes, please come, Nell.' Mark caught her hand. 'I told Aunty Jenny what good fun we had when we went sailing last time, and she said we could borrow a boat and go out on the sea. But she said we were to be sure to bring you, too. So you will come, won't you—please?' He gave her an anxious look, Jenny's well-meaning effort to promote Ben's romance sounding like a condition to his young ears.

'Of course she's coming,' Ben said firmly, a grim challenge in the grey eyes that met hers. 'She wouldn't miss it for the world.' He turned to Mark and said quickly, 'Your friends should be here any minute; why don't you go and look for them?'

Mark ran off, eager to tell his friends about the projected trip. Nell gave Ben an angry look. 'Why tell him I'd go? You know I won't.'

'You're coming,' Ben said shortly.

'I've already made arrangements for the weekend.'

'Liar.'

Getting desperate, Nell said forcefully, 'Look, get it into your head, will you? It's over, finished! We're through. Do I have to spell it out to you?'

'To me, no, I've already got the message loud and clear. But can you tell Mark that you don't have time for him any more? Can you tell a child who's been through all that he's been through, who's just starting to open up with you and like you—can you tell him that you're dumping him, too?'

'That's moral blackmail,' she protested.

'How would you know? You don't have any morals.'

That, and the look Ben gave her when he said it, hurt, hurt unbearably. Her heart raw, Nell's chin came up and she said, 'There's no way I'm going with you.'

'OK. Go and tell Mark that the weekend's off.'

'You and he can still go.'

'You heard Mark; Jenny has invited us all along.' He gave a wintry smile. 'She wants to give us an opportunity to be together, and she wants to get to know you better. The whole weekend has been planned principally for your benefit, so if you don't go none of us goes.'

'That's ridiculous. Why didn't you tell her that it's over between us?'

'Because Mark answered the phone and she told him all about it before I spoke to her. And I didn't see why he should have his enjoyment spoilt just because you're so damn selfish.'

'Selfish?'

'Yes, too selfish to share your life, and too damn selfish to want to take any responsibility.'

Getting desperate, knowing that to spend the weekend with them in these circumstances would be unbearable, Nell said in a fierce undertone, 'I don't want to be a second wife. I don't want to be a stepmother.'

'Coward!' She raised her hand to hit him at that, but Ben caught her wrist and glared down at her. 'And anyway the offer's no longer open.'

'So why insist that I go along?'

'Because I'm not going to have Mark upset again. You're going with us this weekend. And you're going to be nice and friendly until we've finished this collaboration. Then I'm going to take Mark on holiday and you can disappear back into the concrete fall-out shelter you've built round yourself.'

'You don't have to be so nasty. I kept my side of the bargain; it was you who broke it.'

'By falling in love with you? That certainly was a mistake—to fall for an iron-hearted little bitch like you.' Ben gave a grim smile. 'All I hope is that when you finally fall in love yourself that the man kicks you in the teeth, tells you he doesn't want to know. Then maybe you'll learn how it feels.'

Nell looked away, her face set, and it was several long seconds before she said, 'When we've finished the script and you go away, what will you tell Mark about me? What explanation will you give?'

'What the hell do you care?' She flinched and he saw it. And Ben's eyes narrowed as he added, 'That you've gone to work abroad, most probably.'

There was a shout from upstairs and then Mark and his two friends, who had arrived when Ben and Nell were arguing, came down to get the popcorn.

Ben led the way to his workroom and Nell tried to lose herself in the script, but could think of nothing but her own problems. When they broke for lunch she said, 'Where are you going for the weekend?'

'*We* are going to Salcombe, in Devon. Sean and Jenny have a cottage there.'

'And what are the—the sleeping arrangements?'

Ben shrugged. 'I have no idea. It's up to Jenny.'

'But you've been there before; you must know how many bedrooms there are,' she pointed out acidly.

'I don't know what her arrangements are; sometimes the children sleep out in a tent if the weather's fine.'

It was such an ambiguous answer that Nell didn't trust it. She made up her mind that she wouldn't go. It was just too much to ask, more than she could bear. But she let them both believe that she would go and somehow got through the rest of that day. The next day was Friday, the eve of the proposed trip. There was tension in the air from the moment she arrived at Ben's place, and it grew worse as the day wore on. Nell guessed that Ben was just waiting for her to make some excuse to avoid the weekend and was all set to pounce on her, to call her a coward again and force her to go.

So she made no excuse, even smiling and encouraging Mark when he talked excitedly about the outing. When they packed up work for the day she said, 'What time do you want to leave tomorrow?'

'Early. Six o'clock.'

'OK, I'll be here.'

'Oh, no. We'll pick you up.'

Nell shrugged, trying not to show her dismay, having fully intended not to show up. 'There doesn't seem much point in your coming into London and getting snarled up in the traffic. I can easily get a cab out here.'

'And just as easily not get one.' Ben caught her wrist and glared down at her. 'You little coward, do you think I don't see through you? You're coming, even if I have to break down your door and drag you out. Do you understand?'

But Nell could hit back when the stakes were high enough. Wrenching her hand free, she said, 'Oh, sure. Just don't be surprised if you find someone with me, that's all.'

For a fraction of a second he didn't understand, but then Ben's face grew so murderous that she hastily let herself out of the front door and ran down the steps. She hurried along the pavement, half afraid that he might come after her, and it was only when she reached the Tube station that Nell dared to turn round and make sure he wasn't there. On the train going home, she sat with her sunglasses on, trying to hide the tears that wouldn't go away. Whatever Ben had felt for her, that last remark had really blown it. He might have despised her for a coward before but now he would really hate her. Which ought to please her, Nell thought bleakly. Wasn't that the whole idea?

But she was too miserable to sleep that night, didn't even bother to go to bed, and was ready and waiting when Ben rang her bell the next morning.

His eyebrows rose when he saw that she was ready, dressed in white jeans and a sweater, a holdall in her hand. 'Let's go,' she said.

Mark greeted her excitedly from the back seat. It seemed that he hadn't slept much either, but for a very different reason. It was so early that the motorways were clear and they made good time into the West Country, arriving in mid-morning.

Sean and Jenny came to greet them and introduced Nell to Jenny's sister and her husband, who was also down for the weekend with their two children. So the cottage was obviously full and it came as no surprise when Jenny showed them up to a bedroom that she expected them to share, because it contained only a large double bed.

'I don't want to sleep with you,' Nell said tonelessly when Jenny had gone.

'So what's new?'

'So tell her we want separate rooms!' Nell rounded on him angrily. 'Explain.'

'You're the one who wants a separate room; you go and explain.'

'Look, I didn't want to come here. I'm only doing it for Mark's sake. The least you could do is make it easier for me.'

'Sorry, I'm not interested in doing anything for you.'

She gave him a fulminating look, then said, 'Get out while I change.'

For a moment she thought Ben was going to argue, but then he turned and went out. Quickly she changed into a shirt and shorts, put on a pair of yellow canvas espadrilles, pulling the things out of her bag, leaving her other clothes lying on the floor, for once in her life not caring.

Ben had been helping Mark to change in a bedroom that all the children were sharing, then he changed too, and when he was ready they joined the others and all walked down to the seafront. Sean and Jenny had their own sailing dinghy and they'd borrowed a couple of others from friends, so each family had their own.

The three of them got into their dinghy and were pushed off, Mark bouncing up and down on the wooden seat excitedly. 'Put his life-jacket on,' Ben instructed. 'Mark, you sit on that seat and keep still, do you understand?'

Nell pulled a life-jacket out from under the seat and strapped Mark into it, then put one on herself. 'Is there another jacket up your end?' she asked Ben. 'I can only find two.'

He looked and then shrugged. 'The owners must only have two. Not to worry.' He had got the sail up and was concentrating on steering as they headed out into the open sea.

They sailed near the shore, Ben getting the hang of the boat. The others came up and Sean suggested a race. 'See those two buoys out there?' he yelled. 'The first to go round them three times is the winner.'

'A race! A race!' Mark shouted excitedly. 'Come on, Dad, let's win.'

They all sailed up to the starting point, Sean yelled, 'Go!' and they all entered into the spirit of it, leaning to take the boats round the buoys, using tiller and sail to go as fast as possible.

'Come on, Dad! They're winning, they're winning!' Mark was jumping up and down, pointing to the boats in front. Nell had never been in a small boat on the sea before and was beginning to feel a bit queasy. She tried to obey Ben's shouted commands to pull on this rope or that but at one point had to fight off a definite feeling of nausea and didn't pull the rope in time when they were rounding a buoy.

'I'll get it.' Mark gave a shout, jumped up from the seat from which he'd been ordered not to move, and went to reach it.

'Look out!' Ben's frightened yell made Nell quickly look up. The boom was being driven across by the strong wind—but Mark was in the way, his little body in the path of the heavy, swinging beam as he grabbed for the rope.

Without thinking about it, Nell reached out and grabbed the boy's legs, pulled him off his balance so that he fell into the bottom of the boat. But Ben, too, had been trying to save him and had leapt forward. But he'd also let go the tiller and the boom immediately swung back, hit him on the head and knocked him overboard into the water.

'Ben!' Nell screamed out his name. But she had seen his eyes close as he went into the sea and knew he was unconscious. Without hesitation she pulled off her lifejacket so that she could dive and went in after him.

She had to dive deep before she found him and when she got him to the surface the boat was some distance away. The other boats didn't seem to have noticed what had happened and were still racing up to the last buoy, nearly a mile away.

'Mark, over here. Bring the boat over here. Come on.' But the boy was standing staring at them, his whole body rigid. 'I've got him. Come on,' Nell yelled again, her arms aching as she struggled to keep Ben's head out of the waves. But still Mark just stood there.

Suddenly Nell understood. It was his mother's accident all over again. He had been told he'd caused that and now he was afraid that he'd killed his father, too.

'Mark, you've got to help me,' she yelled desperately. 'Come on, sweetie. It's not your fault. It was an accident. You've got to help me; I can't manage alone. Help me, Mark.'

Something in her voice must have got through to him, because the boy suddenly jumped to the tiller and steered towards them, catching the flapping sail so that it filled with wind.

'Oh, you beauty! That's it. Come on.' He got nearer but couldn't manoeuvre the boat close enough. 'Throw me a rope. That's it.' The first time it was short and he had to turn the boat, tack and come back, throw the rope again. This time Nell managed to catch it and pull herself alongside. 'Oh, well done, Mark. Well done!'

'Is he dead? Is he dead?'

His wail of terror made her say sharply, 'No, of course he isn't. You've saved him. You brought the boat back and you've saved him.'

The boy blinked back his tears. 'Can we pull him in?' he asked anxiously, his terrified little face peering over the side.

'No, he's too heavy. But we'll put the life-jacket on him and then tie him to the side. But you'll have to help me.'

Between them they managed it, putting the rope under Ben's armpits and tying it to the side so that he was suspended out of the water, facing the sea, his head lolling on his chest. Nell was alongside him, hoisting him as high as she could so that the boat wouldn't tip with his weight all on one side.

'What shall we do now?' Mark said anxiously.

Nell managed to give him a grin. 'Head for the shore, Captain.'

Mark blinked at her, then to her amazement gave her the travesty of a smile.

The other boats had noticed them now, were coming back. After a few minutes Ben groaned and retched. He tried to move but Nell told him sharply to keep still. He opened his eyes, realised where he was and said, 'What the hell . . . ?'

'It's a new type of game,' Nell told him.

He blinked, remembered and said sharply, fear in his voice, 'Mark?'

He tried to look round but Nell said, 'He's fine. Who do you think is steering the boat?'

'What happened?'

'The boom hit you. Don't worry, you'll be OK.'

'I was knocked out?' She didn't answer and he said, 'You came in after me. You saved my life.'

'Well, I couldn't let you die; we haven't finished our collaboration yet.' Nell tried to speak lightly, but she was clinging to the rope as she supported him and her face was very close to his. Ben looked into her eyes and she had no place to hide, couldn't disguise the love that shone in her face.

'You love me,' he said with certainty. 'I *knew* you loved me.'

Nell sighed and gave up pretending. 'Chauvinist,' she said, and kissed him.

The moon turned the sea to silver, the stars were like velvet in the night sky. Ben came up behind Nell as she stood at the window. He had done that before, only a few nights ago, and it had led to the most wonderful lovemaking she had ever known. But that night seemed like a lifetime ago, so much had happened since. Now he drew her into the room and turned her to face him.

'You have some explaining to do,' he reminded her.

'Yes.'

Nell went and sat on the bed, pulled her knees up and rested her chin on them. The excitement of their boating mishap was over, the whole incident played down except for Mark's part in it. The child now thought himself very brave and clever and he had actually given Nell a hug and a kiss before going to bed that night. But now she had to explain, and it would be entirely dependent on Ben's reaction what would happen next.

'I love you very much,' she told him. 'But I had to make you hate me because—because I was afraid that if I married you you might one day be hurt very badly, both you and Mark.'

Ben sat down on the bed and looked into her face. 'Tell me,' he commanded.

'It was because of something that happened in my past.' Slowly, with many hesitations, she told him the whole sordid story. 'So you see,' she said, finding the words hard to say, 'I've had a child.'

He didn't speak and she raised her eyes to look at him, sure that she would see repulsion in his face. But he said, 'Yes, I know.'

Nell gave him a stunned look. 'But—but how do you know? How can you possibly know?'

He gave a small smile. 'I've known from the first time we made love. You have stretch marks in your skin.'

'Oh! Oh.' She swallowed, and had to think about that before she said, 'Why didn't you ask me about them?'

'I figured you'd tell me when you were good and ready.'

'Oh, Ben.' She gave him a look of wonder and gratitude, but then gritted her teeth and said firmly, 'But I gave my baby away.'

'So what else could you do at eighteen?' Ben said calmly.

'You're—you're not disgusted?'

An amazed look came into his eyes. 'Why on earth should I be? Is that why you tried to turn me against you? Just for that?'

'No, not just for that.' Nell took a deep breath. 'You see, I'm very much afraid that—that Mark is my son.'

Ben's jaw dropped. 'You think...'

'Yes. And I didn't want you to find out and think I'd married you to be near him. Mark might have gone looking for his real mother when he was eighteen and found out it was me, and you might have hated me because——'

'Nell!' Ben caught hold of her shoulders and shook her. 'Are you saying that you did all this because you didn't want to hurt me?'

She nodded, her eyes searching his face.

'Oh, my darling girl. As if I could hate you! Even when you tried so hard to ditch me I still loved you. Somehow I knew that you didn't mean it, and I was hoping against all hope that we could sort it out.'

'But you haven't realised yet,' Nell said forcefully. '*I think Mark is my son.*'

Ben looked at her and to her consternation began to laugh. Taking her in his arms, he said, 'My darling idiot. If that was what you thought why didn't you ask me? We met Mark's mother before we adopted him. She was a student from York University. A very nice girl who'd made a mistake and had enough guts to go through with having the baby and letting it go to a good home rather than have an abortion. Just as you did. No, my darling, I'm sorry, but Mark isn't your son.'

She stared, not sure how she felt. 'You're absolutely sure?'

'Absolutely. You'll just have to love him for himself.'

'Oh, I already do.' Nell wiped away tears of both relief and regret. 'I wish I had asked you, but I could never bring myself to do it in case you told me what you thought of me.'

'Idiot. So have we got all that sorted out now?'

'Oh, yes.'

'Well, thank goodness for that. And do I take it that you do love me, after all?'

'Oh, *yes*, I most certainly do.'

'Then come here, my darling, my love, and show me how much.'

Nell woke in the night, stirred and felt the movement of a body sliding into the bed. She smiled. 'Goodnight, Mark.'

'Goodnight, Nell,' her future stepson answered happily.

Full of Eastern Passion...

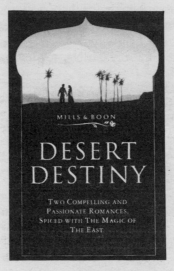

MILLS & BOON

DESERT DESTINY

TWO COMPELLING AND
PASSIONATE ROMANCES,
SPICED WITH THE MAGIC OF
THE EAST.

Savour the romance of the East this summer with
our two full-length compelling Romances,
wrapped together in one exciting volume.

AVAILABLE FROM 29 JULY 1994 PRICED £3.99

MILLS & BOON

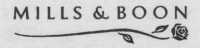

Accept 4 FREE Romances and 2 FREE gifts

FROM READER SERVICE

Here's an irresistible invitation from Mills & Boon. Please accept our offer of 4 FREE Romances, a CUDDLY TEDDY and a special MYSTERY GIFT! Then, if you choose, go on to enjoy 6 captivating Romances every month for just £1.90 each, postage and packing FREE. Plus our FREE Newsletter with author news, competitions and much more.

Send the coupon below to: Mills & Boon Reader Service, FREEPOST, PO Box 236, Croydon, Surrey CR9 9EL.

NO STAMP REQUIRED

Yes! Please rush me 4 FREE Romances and 2 FREE gifts! Please also reserve me a Reader Service subscription. If I decide to subscribe I can look forward to receiving 6 brand new Romances for just £11.40 each month, post and packing FREE. If I decide not to subscribe I shall write to you within 10 days - I can keep the free books and gifts whatever I choose. I may cancel or suspend my subscription at any time. I am over 18 years of age.

Ms/Mrs/Miss/Mr _____ EP70R

Address _____

_____

Postcode _____ Signature _____

mps MAILING PREFERENCE SERVICE